Wild n Free Forever

A collection of winning wild animal
stories by children

For all wild animals – who deserve to be free

Paws n Claws Publishing ©

Using the written word to keep animals in the wild

PAWS N CLAWS PUBLISHING

Paws n Claws Publishing, Canvey Island, Essex

www.pawsnclawspublishing.co.uk

This book copyright ©Paws n Claws Publishing 2014
First edition published 2014 by Paws n Claws Publishing

Edited by Debz Hobbs-Wyatt
Designed and Typeset by *www.lksdesigns.co.uk*

British Library Cataloguing in Publication Data
A Record of this Publication is available from the British Library

ISBN 978-0-9568939-7-0

All Paws n Claws books are published on paper derived from
sustainable resources

Acknowledgements

This is the third collection of stories by children in the *Wild n Free* series. It goes without saying that many people are involved in putting a project like this together, from the schools and the charity that helped promote the competition, through to our lovely graphic designer, Lisa Simmonds, for putting together yet another special book.

Once again it is not possible without our team of judges, all talented writers, who helped to select the shortlist: Carol, Dulcie, Holly, Gill, Julie-Ann, Kirsty, Paula, Pauline and Pat. And then to this year's final judges: Michaela Strachan, Sally Spedding and Kate Tenbeth for choosing the overall winners.

I also want to thank Colin and Justin Wyatt, our artists, for helping to select the drawings – again!

Thanks to Born Free for their support throughout and to all of the children and their families for helping me bring it all together. This has been a wonderful experience and one I hope to repeat again.

Debz

The Born Free Foundation is an international wildlife charity founded by Virginia McKenna, Bill Travers and their eldest son Will Travers, following Bill and Virginia's starring roles in the classic film *Born Free*. Today, headed by their son Will Travers, the Foundation is devoted to wild animal welfare and compassionate conservation, working to save animal lives, stop suffering, rescue individuals and protect rare species. Our charity is determined to end captive animal exploitation, phase out zoos and keep wildlife in the wild. We take action for lions, elephants, gorillas, tigers, wolves, bears, dolphins, turtles and many other species and work with local communities to find solutions to help people and wildlife live together without conflict.

Find out more and get involved at
www.bornfree.org.uk

Born Free Foundation
Broadlands Business Campus, Langhurstwood Road,
Horsham, West Sussex, RH12 4QP, UK
Charity Reg. No. 1070906

Contents

Foreword by Debz Hobbs-Wyatt   IX

A Note about the Cover –
Mother and Baby Giraffe by *Morgan Joy Ashby*   XIII

Years 5 and 6, a note from our judge, Kate Tenbeth   XV

An Old Galápagos Tortoise's Thoughts – *Xander Cleak*   I
Dolphin Encounter – *Tristan Warnock*   4
DRAWING: Dolphins Playing – *Morgan Joy Ashby*   8
A Turtle's Shell – *Daisy Cuthbert*   9
The Fig Tree – *Charlie Aldridge-Bate*   14
Survival Beyond Belief – *Adam Amrani*   17
DRAWING: Fennec Fox – *Adam Amrani*   20
Life is Different in the Murky Depths of the Sea – *Sophien Amrani*   21
DRAWING: Blue-ringed Octopus – *Sophien Amrani*   24
The Platypus – *Thomas Cumming*   26
DRAWING: Duck-billed Platypus – *Thomas Cumming*   28
The Cheetah – *Jack Forshew*   29
The Little African Elephant Calf – *Tristan Hartwell*   32
It's a Rat's Life – *Teddy Jenkins*   35
Courage – *Emma McCarthy*   38
The Lethal Royal Bengal Tiger – *Vivek Nair*   41
DRAWING: Royal Bengal Tiger – *Vivek Nair*   43

Years 7 and 8, a note from our judge, Sally Spedding 45

Howl to Save a Life – *Maia Freeman* 47
DRAWING: Wolf – *Nicole Radtke* 50
Saving Atiya – *Vienna Cooper* 51
A Monkey's Tale – *Alex Cumming* 57
Soot – *Henry Gadsdon* 60
The Creature and the Foal – *Honey Hilton* 63
DRAWING: Zebra – *Morgan Joy Ashby* 65
A Mud Bath – *Tayin Lakhani* 66
The Elusive *Panthera uncia* – *Manas Madan* 69
DRAWING: Black Panther – *Tayin Lakhani* 75
Hope – *Ryan Ratnam* 77
The Story of a Real Hunter – *Thomas Rochussen* 83
An Elephant's Journey – *Lakshman Samarakoon* 87
DRAWING: Orcas – *Mairi Clayton* 90
The Leopard – *Wynn Thomas* 93

Years 9-11, a note from our judge, Michaela Strachan 96

Wriggling away from Wombattiness – *Marisa Orton* 98
The Tigress – *Emily Wootton* 103
DRAWING: Tiger – *Liah Clayton* 105
Snow Baby – *Bethany Dale* 107
The Hunt – *Keira Layton* 111
DRAWING: Tiger – *Morgan Joy Ashby* 115
Goshawk – Life in the Trees – *Dominik Reynolds* 116

The Paws Writing Competition – your chance to be published 122
Paws for Thought Discussion Points – a note for teachers
   and parents 123
Index 125
Other books by Paws n Claws that help wild animals 126
Other books you might enjoy 129

Foreword

When I started the *Wild n Free* series I had two aims – one was to encourage children to think about the lives of wild animals responsibly – to re-examine the role zoos have in modern life, and the second was to encourage children with a writing talent that if I could do it – they could too. In fact my writing ambitions started as a child, aged ten, when I won a writing competition like this one. My story was called *How the Butterfly Got its Colours,* I still have it. It marked the beginning of a journey that eventually led me to work as an editor, a publisher and now a published novelist and short story writer.

The Paws Animal Writing Competition was born not long after I set up Paws n Claws Publishing. This little press has always been about publishing animal stories that will help real wild animals. Some of you might have seen the picture book *Jet-Set* series we created aimed at the little ones. It came after another of my projects, with Bridge House Publishing, when we successfully published a collection of wild animal stories for adults called *Gentle Footprints* in 2010 that was launched at the Hay Festival by none other than founder and trustee of Born Free, actress, Virginia McKenna OBE, now a dear friend.

I had a vision that education about the way we treat animals begins as children; I know it did for me. And that young talent simply must be nurtured. In a world where we cannot even treat fellow humans with kindness, amid terrible wars, children are the key to securing the future of the planet. We also see in the news how literacy is waning today, children read fewer books, and yet in developing nations we also hear how eBooks are cheaper and more accessible to children than running water! What madness. But I know children can see how we treat the planet, I know from the children I meet and the things they say to me. And I also know there is tremendous writing talent out there. This is evident in all the entries we received, even those we were not able to publish here. It is my belief that short stories are a wonderful way, in only a few words, to really connect to a reader and say something important.

I worked as a scientist for a number of years before I became a full time writer. In 2013 I won the Bath Short Story Award and my first novel *While No One Was Watching* was published by Parthian Books. In fact I now have a literary agent in London. So sometimes those dreams we have as children do come true – if you work hard. And believe.

I write to change the way people think, albeit in a small way, and that's what I hope all of the stories here will do for you. Sadly wild animals are still exploited by humans for circuses, dolphinariums and the tourist trade where people have photographs taken with wild animals 'owned' and exploited by people trying to make money. Even today many of us still visit zoos and wildlife parks where animals live in conditions far removed to those in the wild. Many zoos are not there with a primary role to educate and protect animals, but businesses that use animals as exhibits, an old-fashioned idea now we're able to travel to them or see them on documentaries. Times have changed and we must too. Some of you may still like to visit zoos, but all I urge is you take a look at Born Free's website before you do and look at the 'real' facts about animals and what zoos and wildlife parks 'really' contribute to conservation. It can be tough reading. And the message about freedom is one I know I read in every story submitted to this competition. Why is this so important? I'll tell you why – because it's the children who will influence the laws and decisions made in the future – they are the next generation of adults, and the fate of animals, and how we regard them, lies in their hands.

The stories you will read here are the judges' final shortlist, including of course the winner and runner-up in each of the three age categories. Every one of these stories has something special that might just make a difference; and might change attitudes and behaviour towards wild animals. The same message is also depicted so well in the drawings by our talented young artists.

So I will leave you with the message I think myself and all of the children want to make: animals should be born, live and die free.

Let's hope that dream will one day come true as well.

About Debz

Debz Hobbs-Wyatt is a full time fiction writer, editor and publisher. She lives with her cats, Cagney and Lacey, and her mad cocker spaniel, Rosie. She originally trained and worked as a scientist and has a BSc in Zoology and an MSc in Ecology. She has always been passionate about animals. She now has her MA in Creative Writing and works with a lot of developing writers including running PAWS workshops in schools.

Debz has had several short stories published, won the Bath Short Story Award 2013 and was shortlisted in the Commonwealth Short Story Prize 2013. She has written four novels. Her debut novel, *While No One Was Watching*, an adult psychological thriller about a little girl who disappears from the grassy knoll at the exact moment in time President Kennedy is assassinated, was published by Parthian Books in November 2013. She is also an Editor and Publicist for *Bridge House Publishing*, short story specialists; Editor for *CaféLit*, an online short story community; and the founder of *Paws n Claws Publishing*. She writes a daily writing Blog for developing writers.

Useful links

www.debzhobbs-wyatt.co.uk
Twitter: @PawsDebz @DebzHobbsWyatt
Writing Blog: *http://wordznerd.wordpress.com*
www.pawsnclawspublishing.co.uk
www.thejet-set.com

A Note about the Cover

Mother and Baby Giraffe by *Morgan Joy Ashby*

We had so many wonderful drawings to choose from, and the pleasure of choosing which ones made it into the book and onto the cover fell to our professional artists: Colin and Justin Wyatt.

They did a great job.

Colin said, *"We were impressed with the drawings – the children had clearly taken a lot of time and paid attention to detail to really capture the animals. All we did was select our favourites for the book. But then we had to decide about the cover. Well actually it was an easy decision in the end. We both whole-heatedly agreed that Morgan's giraffes would make a wonderful eye-catching cover! Well done."*

There are several of Morgan's drawings throughout the book, so look out for them!

About the cover artist

Morgan Joy Ashby was twelve when she did all of her illustrations. She would like to thank her wonderful mother for such a free-range life, with lots of nature, art, music, craft, stories, beaches, adventures, museums, castles, camps, horses… lots of learning and no school. Morgan has had artwork published before by *Young Writer*, *Writers' Forum*, *Animal Action* and *Picturehouse Cinemas*. Morgan loves all animals, she's vegetarian, and has been especially inspired by visiting the Cairngorm reindeer and by watching the foals Willow and Rowan growing up at Jane's stables. David Attenborough's wildlife films have also helped deepen her understanding of evolution and far-away habitats.

Years 5 and 6

A note from our judge, Kate Tenbeth

Kate Tenbeth is an established children's writer, author of *Burly and Grum Tales* and a young adult book called *Unlucky Dip*. She says just can't stop writing! She's had a varied career, having worked in news and current affairs (Radio 4 and *The Economist*) in London and also in a scuba diving shop in the West Indies. Her ideal environment would be to live in a cake shop on the beach and write whatever she likes for the rest of her life! Maybe one day...

Meanwhile, she commutes into London every day and writes in the evening. Find out more about her here on her website: *www.burlyandgrum.com*. You will also find her books being sold on the Born Free website.

This is what she had to say about the stories:

"I was very impressed by the standard of writing and the level of knowledge that each child showed about the animal they had chosen to write a story about. They should all be very proud of their work. In fact I ended up choosing joint winners as the stories were so good.

Dolphin Encounter is an adventurous and exciting story and a worthy joint winner. Tristan Warnock uses very descriptive writing. His love and knowledge of marine life is obvious and he shows understanding that wild creatures belong in the wild. The story is well constructed, i.e. it has a solid introduction which leads to an exciting adventure and then progresses to a well-thought-out ending.

In An Old Galápagos Tortoise's Thoughts by Xander Cleak, I just fell in love with the character of Boris, the cranky old tortoise from the Galápagos Islands. Boris reflects on the way the relationship between tortoise and human has changed over the years. It's a story that is observant and humorous but also very poignant. Xander has obviously researched the history of the Galápagos Islands and tortoises and has an understanding of the impact that humans can have, both good and bad, on wildlife. And hence my joint winner. I just couldn't choose one over the other!

I chose A Turtle's Shell by Daisy Cuthbert as my second place because Shelly is a tenacious (and very hungry!) turtle who goes on a journey that is packed with adventure. Daisy knows a lot about turtles, how they hunt for food and why they go on difficult and dangerous journeys, and she has managed to convey a lot of information in a fun way – you have to keep reading to find out what happens to Shelly!"

The winning stories and all the runners-up follow. I wonder if you will have the same favourites as our judges?

Winning Stories: Years 5 and 6 Joint Winner

An Old Galápagos Tortoise's Thoughts
Xander Cleak

There are lots of people about today. They chatter, chatter, and are so loud even when they think they're being quiet. Or it might be just that the sounds they make don't belong here. My kind have long memories. We've seen the smiles that are different to the smiles the people wear today; the smiles that are hungry to taste our blood and flesh. And we remember the faces that don't smile, that don't care, they're too busy clearing our land away to make way for the oinks of their pigs and the bleating of their goats. Not to mention the dogs they bring with the sharp teeth who want to get inside our shells. Too many of my cousins aren't here to make new memories of the humans with kinder faces, who just want to make pictures of us, and count us, and measure us. They laugh being around us as if they have always been our friends. But they have short lives so maybe they don't remember the things that we remember.

Personally I don't mind the humans. They can be a pleasant diversion between eating and sleeping. Not as pleasant as a nice wallow in a muddy pool, but they're still fine. Although I do prefer the finches and mockingbirds. All I have to do is raise up on my legs and stretch my neck out and they'll peck all the nasty little ticks off my body.

A perfect relationship, and we understand each other wonderfully without any need for all the noisy chatter of the humans.

Today the humans are talking extra lots.

"You're getting old, Boris," they say after examining my shell. (Boris is what some of the humans call me for some reason, but a wise tortoise once told me that humans don't eat things they give names to, so I shouldn't complain.)

Hmmmph. I know that, I don't need any pink-skinned young thing of a human to tell me that. Humans rush through life like it doesn't matter, but still they think they can comment on my age.

And I am even older than the numbers they discuss and scribble on their bits of paper. The nerve of it, calling me old and not even getting their facts right. I bite the legs of the nearest one.

The humans laugh.

"Ah, it's so cute. He likes you, he really likes you," one of the humans says.

For a moment I wish I was one of the dogs. But bigger and with sharper teeth.

I'm too old to get angry or want a different life though, I go back to nibbling on grass which is much nicer than human leg anyway and let the humans do whatever they want to do.

I know I am going to die soon. Often old ones like me come to an end in silly accidents like falling off the side of a mountain we've known all our lives. I don't mind that too much, it's a bit of drama at the end of a long life, something for the grandchildren to tell stories about. But I wish I could stretch out my neck and make the humans understand what I want. I've tried before, and sadly although the birds are smart enough to communicate with us, humans aren't smart enough to understand. I'd like peace on my island. I'd like the world back to the stories my grandparents told me, when there were so many of us and nothing to hurt us.

Even though I don't mind them, I still wish the humans would go away and not come back.

Then I watch the humans, they're doing something different to normal. From somewhere, as if by magic, they've produced lots of young tortoises. Eggs that went missing years ago are returned to us as new, beautiful friends.

I smile. Maybe humans can stay around after all. Maybe they'll be our saviours not our destroyers.

About the author

Xander Cleak goes to St Birinus School in Dorchester-On-Thames. His favourite subjects are maths and reading time. He likes action books and *Just William* stories. He doesn't like playing the piano but is persevering with it, and has taken his grade two exam. He prefers singing and dancing to jazz and Yazoo songs.

His big aim is to design amazing computer games that everyone loves and to save the rainforest.

This story is dedicated to Nanny Dotto who loves all animals and helps to look after their old dog Morty.

Joint Winner

Dolphin Encounter
Tristan Warnock

The view before my eyes was picturesque. I had woken up from my deep sleep in a tourist boat on the Atlantic Ocean, off the Isles of Scilly, and peered out of the porthole sleepily. The Scilly Isles are a tiny group of islands situated twenty-eight miles off Land's End and are a sanctuary for wildlife. I had spent many a happy childhood holiday on one of the islands called Tresco and it had always been my dream to spend a week on a boat observing the marine life around the islands because I wanted to be a marine biologist when I grew up, studying and protecting marine animals in the wild.

The sun shone like a pale golden coin suspended in the sky and the sea was a deep inky blue. All of a sudden, out of the swell, a pod of dolphins accelerated at the front of our boat in the bow wave. The captain slowed the boat down gradually and came to a halt so that we could take photos from the deck. For me it was like a wish come true to be that close to a pod of wild dolphins.

I leaned over the guardrail and tried to reach down to stroke a dolphin. I lost my balance and began to topple forwards. An adrenaline surge rushed through my body as I splashed into the salt water. The water was icy cold and

I could hardly move a muscle in my body. I sank slowly towards the seabed and landed in the soft sand below. I opened my eyes and the salt water stung them like lemon juice. It was all blurry.

I could see light above me but all of a sudden a dark shadow hovered overhead and I felt a sharp nudge in my side. It was painful but I thought it was a dolphin coming to rescue me. I had read that dolphins have saved humans from drowning in my *National Geographic* magazines. A very dark thought told me that it was not the dolphin and I soon discovered I was right. It was a huge, aggressive seal and he was circling and coming at me again. A large male seal can kill a man in water. I was terrified.

Suddenly a dolphin streaked past and hit the seal side on. This was no ordinary seal. He was a big strong male and he was protecting his herd. There were females with babies all around on the rocks, which we had come to see. The seal struck back with a bite on the dolphin's side. He had a mouth full of big, sharp teeth. The dolphin suffered a nasty wound and was bleeding but that did not stop him. Somehow it seemed he was trying to protect me. He started circling me to make sure I was untouched. The seal came towards me again. I was scared but the dolphin seemed to swoop down and scoop me up. He was lifting me up towards the light. I reached the surface gasping for air. Everyone on board was screaming by now. A life ring slapped into the water beside me. I grabbed it and was hoisted up and onto the boat. It had all happened so quickly although it had felt like such a long time that I had been in the water.

My mother was crying with joy that I survived and everyone on the boat crowded me. I was wrapped in a foil blanket and I started getting a headache. But this was no time to be hugged by Mum; all I could think of was that incredible dolphin. I forgot my fear and pain and jumped up to look back down into the ocean. The dolphin was still being attacked by the seal and I could see that it was weak from its injury. I gasped and cried out that we needed to help it. This creature had saved me and I was desperate to help it in return. The captain was already radioing the Marine Wildlife Rescue Service.

Meanwhile the rest of the dolphin pod had returned to support the single dolphin who had stayed back to help me. The pod had swum off soon after our boat had stopped, but they must have noticed one was missing or heard him in distress. Dolphins can hear each other's sounds under water from a long way off.

The marine rescue team did not take long to arrive and the injured dolphin was lifted into a special cradle and carefully taken to the nearby marine wildlife sanctuary, where he was taken care of by experts. I asked to visit him regularly during the rest of my holiday and learned a lot about dolphins. The marine vets were committed to getting him back into the sea as quickly as possible, but not until they knew he was safe and fully able to look after himself and survive in his natural habitat.

I had been involved in a serious encounter with a wild dolphin that I would never forget. I followed the dolphin's recovery and progress and was lucky enough to be there when he was released back into the ocean where he belonged. He looked happy as he swam away and that made me feel happy too. This beautiful creature had saved my life and I hoped somehow he knew that in return we had also saved his.

About the author

Tristan Warnock is an eleven-year-old boy who lives with his family in Cobham, Surrey. He is a pupil at Cranmore School in West Horsley. Tristan adores animals and has a one-year-old flat coated retriever called Jetson and a three-year-old tortoise called Tex.

Tristan loves marine life and started showing an interest in sharks, whales and dolphins from a very young age. Tristan set his story in the beautiful Isles of Scilly because it's one of his most favourite holiday destinations. It's a very wild 'n' free place with lots of nature.

When he grows up, Tristan wants to be a marine biologist. Tristan would like to dedicate his story to his Omi and Papa (Grandma and Grandpa) because they first took him on holiday to Tresco in the Isles of Scilly which inspired him to write this story.

Paws for Thought Discussion Point

So how many of you made a wish to one day swim with dolphins? It sounds like a great thing to do, doesn't it? Especially if we love animals. What I like so much about Tristan's story is the encounter was natural and the dolphin was later reintroduced to the wild. But a lot of us go on holiday and pay for 'dolphin encounters'. If this is you – please think again. You will read more later about captive dolphins and how Born Free are working hard to stop the exploitation of whales and dolphins in places like SeaWorld. But there is also a tourist industry that allows people like you and I to swim, not only with captive dolphins (taken from the wild), but also in the sea with wild dolphins. If you ever have the opportunity, when swimming or diving, to happen upon a pod of dolphins and get to swim up close

– that would be wonderful. But please don't pay to do this. Dolphins are wild animals and deserve to be left to swim and live freely; not exploited by man. In some places these beautiful creatures are herded and enticed with food so people can swim with them. This is not a natural encounter and can be dangerous. No animal should be exploited for us. And please, please never swim with a captive dolphin. See more on this on page 91.

Dolphins Playing *by Morgan Joy Ashby (cover artist)*

Runner-up

A Turtle's Shell

Daisy Cuthbert

Shelly the loggerhead turtle was lying on her stomach on a small island in the sun when she suddenly felt that she had to go somewhere. She thought it would be a very long and very dangerous journey, but she had to, she was sure she knew where she was to go; she just wasn't sure what place it was.

So she set off on her journey, first wading slowly into the sea and then swimming at top speed, using all four flippers.

She was not very far on her journey when she spotted one of her favourite foods, a huge crab. It was scuttling innocently along the sandy sea floor, looking for some tasty food when Shelly attacked. It was a long and fierce fight, but neither would give up. Shelly was using her strong jaws to try to chew the crab's shell off and the crab was using its claws to try to cut Shelly. In the end Shelly won the fierce fight, but ended up with a cut on her forehead. She crunched on the hard shell of the crab and chewed the insides gently. She took a while to eat it but she knew it would keep her going for a few hours.

***

It was getting late and Shelly's flippers were getting tired so she shuffled around on the sandy sea floor for a bit until she found some soft, dark green seaweed. She pulled it off with her strong jaws and made a seaweed bed on a grey, lumpy rock.

She was a bit hungry so she lay on the rock for a while and waited for something to swim by. It was only a few minutes later when a jellyfish lazily drifted past. She attacked and killed it straight away. She wolfed it down like it was the only meal she had had all day. Then she clambered sleepily into her seaweed bed and was asleep almost instantly.

***

Shelly woke just as the sun was rising, and after a tasty breakfast of fish she was on her way again.

The sun had just made it into the sky when she met a swarm of prawns. They were scuttling and floating around happily when a huge, oval-shaped object blocked out the sunlight. The prawns didn't seem to notice, but Shelly did. She started swimming back the way she'd come. She had almost escaped the dark, looming shadow when she swam into a net. She turned around, but she was too late. The net closed around her and the prawns, they were trapped. She kicked and fidgeted all she could but it was no use, there was no escape. Shelly and the prawns were getting lifted slowly up to the surface of the water. As they were then lowered into a boat, the net opened and men started to pick up the prawns and put them on a conveyor belt.

Shelly fidgeted vigorously until she managed to wriggle out of the pile of prawns. She was shocked when she looked up to see humans standing across from her. Shelly and the humans stared at each other, both shocked. Shelly made the first move, she shuffled to the side of the boat as fast as her flippers would carry her, but she wasn't fast enough. The humans caught her and put her in a wooden box, she tried to escape by wriggling, but it was no use.

"This one will do for the zoo," said one of the humans.

Another said, "I think we'll get a fortune for her."

Then they shut the box and slowly walked away. They all went in different directions, some went to the back of the boat and some went to the front. Shelly suddenly heard a loud, roaring sound, the noise frightened her so she started to wriggle and fidget. She started to feel like she was gliding through the water, the boat was moving.

She flapped her flippers and jumped up and down so much that the box rolled over and the lid opened. It made a big clatter, but she still shuffled out. She was at the side of the boat by now when one of the humans turned around and saw her. She tried to climb over the side but she wasn't tall enough. The human ran towards her but he slipped and fell in the trail of water she had left behind her. Shelly jumped; it might have been the biggest jump she had made in her life. She was frightened she wouldn't make it, but she knew she had to try because if she stayed on the boat she would be taken to the zoo and used for entertainment. While she was thinking about all this she completely forgot she was flying through the air and she landed in the water with a splash. She lay in the water for a few seconds as still as a rock until she realised what had happened.

She was on her way again a few seconds later, and after swimming through what seemed to be a never-ending trail of seaweed, she spotted something that was quite a treat for her. In front of her, flapping their tentacles gently as if they didn't have a care in the world, was a huge swarm of clear, blue jellyfish. Shelly didn't wait for a second, she went straight for the kill, and she sped through the water towards them, leaving a trail of bubbles behind her. They all scattered in different directions, but Shelly didn't care, she went after each of them, using her sharp jaws to catch them and chew them to pieces before swallowing. After that satisfying meal she started to feel a bit tired and her tummy felt unusually heavy.

She looked for some seaweed, ripped it with her strong jaws and made it into a little bed. Before long she was fast asleep.

***

When Shelly woke up bright and early in the morning she started to swim straight away, and it wasn't long before she found her breakfast: a huge, fat, juicy crab. A long fight followed, involving pinching, biting and cracking noises. Shelly was victorious, and won the vicious fight after the crab gave up and tried to scuttle away quickly. Shelly pretended to do the same, but turned around when the crab wasn't looking, swam straight up and along until she was directly above the crab. She darted as fast as lightning, got a direct hit and smashed the crab's shell.

So after a tasty breakfast of crab she was on her way again. Her tummy felt even heavier, and she was sure she recognised her surroundings.

***

As the water got shallower and the waves got smaller Shelly realised where she was going, she was going to a beach to lay her eggs. When she got to the soft, dry sand she shuffled slowly up the small, golden slope and started to dig a hole with her flippers. It was as she was digging she realised where she was, she was at the beach where she was born! She was digging right next to the hole which she came out of when she was a newly hatched turtle.

When she finished digging the hole, she layed her pearly white eggs in it and then shuffled slowly down the flaky sand to the sea. She looked back at her eggs one more time, turned around and then swam into the sea, fighting against the waves until the water was deep enough for her to swim underwater.

***

A few weeks later Shelly's eggs hatched. There were sixteen baby turtles all together. After they had hatched they crawled slowly out of the hole, using their front flippers to pull themselves out. When they were out of the hole they skidded down the little slope on the beach, which felt very steep to the baby turtles. When they finally reached the sea they waded in slowly at first and then started swimming under the water, learning to use their flippers by flapping them and then using them properly. It didn't take them long to get out to sea and before they knew it they were becoming young adults, free to explore the ocean and follow Shelly's unique path.

About the author

Daisy Cuthbert was born in Fife in Scotland and lives in Cardenden with her mum, dad, brother Arran and four crazy springer spaniels: Molly, Archie, Broxi and Blue. Daisy enjoys animal rescue and wildlife programmes and this is how she got the idea for her turtle story. She enjoys Minecraft, anything to do with unicorns and a good giggle with her friends.

Daisy loves reading and writing and would love to be an author. She attends Denend Primary School and would love to be as successful as Ian Rankin who also went there.

Daisy would like to dedicate her story to Great Grandma and Granny Annie who are watching from heaven.

The Fig Tree
Charlie Aldridge-Bate

All I could do was watch as the forest burned down. I was biting back a sob. I had just seen my parents die. The fire was tearing up the rainforest. I didn't know what to do. I felt helpless and lost, just a stray baby gibbon sitting on a burnt leafless branch. I didn't feel like food or drink. It was just me and the grief tugging at my stomach. I just sat there on the branch. Eventually I drifted off to sleep.

***

I woke with a start and realised I was starving. I looked around for a fruit tree. But all the trees had burnt in the fire. I looked around again but I could still not see any fruit trees. I longed for a nice, juicy fig. I started to swing from tree to tree. I swung through the leafless trees for hours. Soon it started to get dark and I found a nice branch to sleep on. I laid down and instantly fell asleep. I woke up and continued to swing. I swung for another couple of hours. Finally I found a small fig tree.

***

I loved figs. When I was little, Mom and Dad would bring me loads. We would feast for hours, digging our teeth into the juicy fruit. Thinking about my parents made me sad. I tried to put them out of my head. I was just about to swing to the fig tree when I realised that there was a

14

family of leopards around the trunk. I was fast but I was not as fast as a leopard – and they could climb!

I felt ashamed of myself. My dad could have easily got to the figs but I was scared out of my skin. Once again I felt helpless and small. But suddenly I had an idea. I might not be as fast as the male of the family but I was faster than the cubs. I would wait until the adults went to fetch water and would quickly run and get some figs for myself.

I waited all morning but the leopards stayed put. Eventually the larger leopards left for the river, leaving their little ones in the shade. I jumped for the tree, grabbed some figs and some leaves to suck water from. I swung up and well away.

That night I feasted on the figs I had grabbed, and sucked on the leaves I had collected. I was planning on eating the figs all by myself but when I saw the baby gibbon, so small like I had been; I couldn't just let her starve. I swung over to her with a fig in my hand and gave it to her. She took it and started to chew. As she got to the middle she started to chew more confidently and faster. She (I guessed it was a she) put out her hand as if to say she wanted more. I went over to my pile of figs handed her one and once again she chewed with hunger. "Thank you," she whispered quietly.

"Come with me," I replied. I cradled her into my arms and we swung off into the forest.

About the author

Charlie Aldridge-Bate was born in Guildford in 2004 and has attended Cranmore School in West Horsley since he was four years old. His favourite subjects at school are English and

P.E. Charlie loves playing football with his two brothers and is a keen skier. He is also an avid reader and enjoys fantasy and adventure novels such as *Artemis Fowl, Harry Potter* and the *Chronicles of Ancient Darkness.*

Charlie got the inspiration for his story *The Fig Tree* when he was reading the Michael Morpurgo book *Running Wild.*

He doesn't quite know what he wants to be when he grows up yet but being an author doesn't sound like a bad idea!

Survival Beyond Belief

Adam Amrani

Scurrying around on the piping hot sand, I leapt onto a slightly cooler surface on a rock. I scanned my forsaken surroundings of the cosmic Sahara Desert; I looked at a rustling in a thorny bush cautiously. Then, there was dead silence. Crawling underneath a towering palm tree, I shook my long and pointed ears to cool me down like a fan. A funny sensation came over me as I felt the starvation in my belly. Remembering my children, who hadn't eaten in days, I knew I had to track down a meal. Hunting in these parts of the desert is always perilous, but a requisite to staying alive. Despite the fact that the chances of finding sustenance in this part of the world are infinitesimal, I still had to find a way. My dingy yellow-coloured fur helped camouflage me as I lay in the golden sand with the sun blazing. Apprehensively and uneasily, I scrambled forward with my bulging eyes looking at the horizon. Alert, I ventured further into this no man's land, encircled by endless sand dunes.

The scorching hot weather burnt me. This is why I prefer to hunt at night as it is cooler and I get more stealth, however, I had no choice as my children had missed too many meals. Staggering on, I sniffed out a miniscule scorpion lying there, I pounced on it! As if it had transformed into a thunderbolt, it threw itself into a nearby crevice. My weakened emaciated legs collapsed suddenly and without warning. Just when I was about to give in to despair, I glimpsed a gloomy hole in the distance. Any prey could be lurking in there. Hope resurfaced in a quick heartbeat. Strong survival instincts made strength flow in my veins again. Willpower took over me as my legs rose to their full height. I then realised that I was unstoppable!

Worming myself through the hole, I saw seven juicy eggs tucked in there. Backing away from the ashen white eggs, I realised this succulent meal would come with a hefty price. A chill ran down my spine as I realised that it was a snake's nest! A mother would put up a fight to protect them as I would my own. But nothing would stop me from fighting to the bitter end either. As I approached the eggs vigilantly, I heard a harsh hiss that reverberated from the back of the hole. A rattle followed as it sent its threatening message. I realised then it was the mighty diamondback rattlesnake! Two diabolical luminous ruby red eyes stared right at me. An evil expression spread across its face. Snarling and bearing my teeth, I tensed my muscles in readiness. Showing off my jaws, I howled and hit it with my claws. Hissing spitefully, it bit me at the side of my neck quickly and precisely injecting its toxic poison. As the neurotoxin begun to kick into me, I became wiry and dizzy. I fell down to the ground! Crash!

Many memories and thoughts were whizzing about in my head like shooting stars zooming around in the night sky. I then questioned myself in my blank mind. Was I still alive? Somehow I felt the poison drain out of my body, but I was still as stiff as a decrepit tree. A thought materialised in my head. I was immune to poison! Suddenly, out of the blue, life burst back into me as a streak of determination ran through me as the thought of my children fuelled my drive to succeed. Springing up from my dead-like form, I dug my claws into the flesh of the unaware snake. Wriggling about, trying to escape my clutch, I inflicted him with my last fatal blow using my mouth to thrash it about frantically.

Scarlet red stained the ground as blood dripped from my mouth. Without any hesitation, I grabbed the eggs and packed them in my mouth. Scrabbling out of the hole, I felt a mix of emotions: joy, pride and triumph. But I quickly realised that my journey back to my den was filled with unspeakable dangers and that I had to get there swiftly and in one piece! I sprinted briskly in an attempt to remain unnoticed.

That didn't last for long. As I passed by a lifeless tree, two scrawny vultures sat there, staring at my hunt prize. A slight leer spread across their faces as they took off and began to circle me. Their sharp talons were great weapons so I had to be vigilant. Hastily, one of them plunged down on me like a spitfire crash landing as it screeched hoarsely. As it spread its claws out, I dived to the side just out of reach and was on the verge of being ambushed before the second vulture was about to saw me in half. I knew that my den was only a few yards away so I assembled my remaining vigour and shot off like a rocket towards it without looking back. In a dream-like fashion, I found myself in my den! In sheer happiness and relief, a few tears trickled down my muzzle. I finally realised that my family will survive for now and that tomorrow would be another day. I am fast, I am invincible, I am the fennec fox!

Fennec Fox *by Adam Amrani*

About the author/artist

Adam Amrani is an eleven-year-old boy who attends St Martin's School in Northwood. His favourite hobby is researching interesting animals. Adam has a pet Gecko named Thunder and is currently trying to convince his parents to adopt a baby bulldog.

The fennec fox caught his eye so he decided to research it to spread other children's awareness. His motivation to write comes from a passionate interest in English and he dedicates this story to Ms Flynn who is an inspiration and his mum Clare who cherishes him.

🐾 Paws for Thought Discussion Point

What can you find out about this interesting creature? Why do you think the fennec fox has such large ears? Is it related to the fox we see in gardens in the UK?

Life is Different in the Murky Depths of the Sea

Sophien Amrani

Four kilometres below the sinister sea, lay my humble dwellings. I am known to everyone as the intoxicating blue-ringed octopus.

My beautiful blue gems on my soft body shine like stars in the enchanted, infinite space. As I wasn't fully awake yet, I lay on a lumpy rock and showed my bright and flamboyant blue rings as a distinct warning to any predator loitering. I was one of those animals that everyone knew to be extremely dangerous. My beige colour with light brown patches meant I could camouflage against my surroundings. Being a soft-bodied creature, I knew I wasn't the only fierce one around. The Angler Fish had troubled my ancestors for decades. They had enormous crescent-shaped mouths, filled with serrated translucent teeth and a piece of dorsal spine placed above their mouths, tipped with a lure of luminous flesh.

I set off hunting for some of my favourite snacks; juicy crabs and shrimps, but I was feeling that famished I would settle for a hermit crab or even a small injured fish. A glowing spotlight caught my eye, but I ignored it and moved on. Swimming along the dark depths of the sea I thought I could make out some shadows. A little bustling shrimp whirled around trying to camouflage, but I could still see its eyes and lungs. In a quick and swift movement I demolished the feisty little creature with my powerful beak. That was a promising start to my hunting journey.

The light caught my attention again, this time I decided to investigate. Piercing objects, that were besmirched shades of yellow, glowed in the farthest distance. I knew immediately then that I was having an encounter with a familiar old enemy, Spike the Angler Fish. With a mighty swing of my delicate curling tentacles I tried to disappear. My father had taught me how to become translucent to avoid my enemy, however, Spike also had evolved to catch her prey and I knew she would use her weapon to glow and track me down.

Squirting ink at Spike I took my chance to escape. Spike clearly hadn't been expecting my counter attack and took a while to recover. I knew I had little time to get out of the danger zone as I was aware she could speed through the waters at twenty-five miles an hour. The Angler Fish was a female, but because she was so tough I gave her the name Spike. Looking back, I saw that she was not far behind me. I turned to the left flank and lured her in towards me. Opening her mouth wide, Spike bit into my supple body. Releasing a deadly level of toxic poison from my blue rings into her mouth, abruptly she let go of me. Luckily, Spike had only pierced a superficial layer of my body and I managed to avoid her razor-sharp teeth. This time I would survive!

Even though seemingly most of my problems vanished with the Angler Fish Spike; having departed from this world, I felt rather remorseful about her demise. After all she was a worthy opponent and was very resilient too. Unfortunately life under these murky waters was hazardous though. It was either Spike or me and this time, I had been the victor. Thinking about my home, I realised that I had lost sight of where I was and only knew I had been pulled along by the tide out of my comfort zone and towards the middle of the Pacific Ocean. As I ventured forward I could just make out a shipwreck in the far distance. I had never come across one of these colossal objects before, but I remember my mother telling me wild stories about large and hazardous wooden transports.

With a mixture of emotions; thrill at the new encounter, trepidation at the unknown and my mother's warnings, I assembled some courage and pushed myself towards the shipwreck to explore the new surroundings.

The blue-green plankton that floated around was demolished by the passing fish as they considered this a delicacy and such easy prey. I marvelled at the way the plankton just appeared to swim straight into the mouths of their enemy! The microscopic crabs particularly enjoyed this banquet as it was a big meal for them. I watched the different variety of sea creatures eat, as if a parent watching over its children. It was quite tempting to grab and devour one of the shrimps, but I felt sorry for them as they had so much stress in their life because of hiding from predators continuously.

"What would it feel like being hunted every single day of your life"? I asked myself. With a quick flash of my tentacles, I disappeared into the far distance. Why was I created if my purpose in life was to frighten the majority of the sea creatures? I was just a scary monster who was self-centred and only thought about himself. It made me feel powerful but also sad that I never really had a true friend as I was seen as such a threat.

The environment around me was very peaceful and it felt good to wallow in my self-pity. My tender head swayed in the gentle and warm current above me. My suckers on my tentacles firmly gripped onto the rock beneath me so that I didn't get washed further away from home. My mind was focused on my poor behaviour towards the other innocent sea creatures. The thought of bullying other creatures made me feel ashamed and sad. "Today," I said aloud to myself, "I will become a better blue-ringed octopus."

I vowed that I would show an act of kindness each day and save my deadly poison for only those who were true enemies. I looked around me and made a promise to myself that I would make these murky waters a happier place to be.

Blue-ringed Octopus *by Sophien Amrani*

About the author/artist

Sophien Amrani is an eleven-year-old boy, who lives in Harrow and goes to St Martin's School in Northwood. His passion is researching animals in factual books and watching animal documentaries.

He has a farm in Marrakesh with many interesting animals.

He wrote about the blue-ringed octopus because of its extraordinary characteristics; such as its supple body and sapphire blue gem rings. His inspirations among many were Ms Flynn, Ms Fair, his mother Clare and his friend Thomas Cumming who is a genius at writing. (His story coincidently is next!)

The Platypus

Thomas Cumming

The blazing ball of fire slowly sinks beneath the tree-tops as blue light shines across my back, reminding me that it is hunting hour. I waddle towards the sand bank, making a useless effort to hide my noisy plodding sound. As the night falls the sand is sparkling in the moonlight, as if tiny diamonds lay concealed in the ground. The black fluid sweeps the bank, pulling small stones and pebbles to the depth. I ruffle my fur and slide into the darkness. The murky water world lay in front of me. The collection of pebbles, gathered by the waves, cobbles the river bed as the seaweed dance with the motion of the river. Surrounding me is all the hidden life of the water.

My feet spread, revealing the webbing in between my claws. The fur on my body suddenly becomes smooth and silky and with a swat of my pancake-flat tail I shoot through the dark. My sensitive bill scans the water, in search of a scent of food. Hair spikes up when a strong smell hits my nose. Paws open, my venomous claw slides from beneath my flesh, ready for the kill. The orange prey floats above my head, as if teasing me. In a quick snap the shrimp is no more. I chew the victim, satisfied with my catch. Suddenly, green seaweed is falling all around me, and distracted by the shrimp, it easily ties all over my body. My limbs toss and turn but the seaweed cuts into me, threatening to knot on my neck. Frustrated by the trap, I tear and thrash at the ropes, desperately trying to escape. Fear strikes me as I realise that I'm imprisoned. I stop squirming and give up, squeaking as loud as I can, hoping something will hear me.

Then huge menacing bars drop from the surface, blocking out all remaining light. Darkness closes around me, until my vision is completely black.

***

My gloved hands reach into the net, hoping that finally there would be something worth eating. I hall out the heavy cage and drag it slowly to the muddy bank. Then much to my surprise, the cage jumps and a squeak comes from within. Carefully, I remove the rusty catch and open the bars. A fluffy ball lies huddled in the corner, enclosed by thick green mesh. My hands slowly seal around the animal and I place it on my lap. Careful not to cut the creature, I snip the cords, and slowly reveal the platypus. A flat, black duck-like bill connects to a brown beaver head. Its paws flop up and down, flashing razor claws at my leg. Its plump body leads to a flat tail, as if designed to swipe flies. I could not help but laugh. Chuckling, I take the animal off my lap and put it on the ground. It clumsily waddles on its knuckles to the bank, its bill sniffing the earth, guiding him to the water. It transforms from a clumsy freak to a majestic seal as soon as it sets foot in the liquid. My eyes follow the creature as it plunges to the darkness. Never in my life had I seen this animal but I can feel the water swelling in my eyes.

"Not much meat on it anyway," I laugh to myself, as I haul the net back in the water.

Duck-billed Platypus *by Thomas Cumming*

About the author

Thomas Cumming is eleven years old and enjoys writing stories and poems. He was very excited when he was told that he had had his work published in a book as he and his class enter every year and until now Thomas has been unsuccessful. He does many things, such as badminton and drawing and lives with his mother, father, older brother and two guinea pigs – Mr Nibbles and Mindy – in Hertfordshire. He goes to St Martin's School, Northwood and is very lucky to have a brilliant and driving English teacher, Ms Flynn. He also has a love of animals, likes reading books of all types and enjoys playing on his brother's Xbox in his spare time.

🐾 Paws for Thought Discussion Point

What a weird and wonderful creature this is! What can you find out about it? Can you find out one peculiar interesting fact about it, and let us know at Paws?

The Cheetah

Jack Forshew

I awoke in my den but my family was fast asleep. I slipped out of the cave and took a look at the vast grassland savannah we live in. I quietly sharpened my semi-retractable claws on the rock walls of our den. We live in Namibia; the place with the largest population of cheetahs in the world.

Even though I was being quiet, my scratching was loud enough to wake my family. Then our mother told us to group around her. She told us that we had to leave her because we had been with her for eighteen months. So we readied ourselves; then our sisters left us first. They each went on their own, then it was time for me and my brothers to leave.

Our mum told us, "You boys need to stick together and form a group called a Coalition and stay close together."

We set out to the part of the savannah where all the longest, juiciest grass was.

We went there because it's where all the antelopes and hares were. But it was also the place where the lions and hyenas were. We had to be careful around them because they are very hostile. We can usually outrun them but we have to be very cautious. We closely surveyed the land and saw no predators but we saw lots of prey. The three of us started running towards the antelopes. We were at sixty miles an hour in three seconds. I ran, leaped, readied my claws and pinned an antelope to the ground. The antelope struggled then finally it stopped moving. Two out of three of us had got food. I had killed an antelope and one of my brothers had killed two hares. We carried the food to a space between some shrubs. Then we found a den there to stay for the night. We ate our food ravenously because we were starving.

We woke up early the next morning, our stomachs rumbling noisily. We silently killed some hares and swallowed them. Suddenly, out of nowhere, a lion came charging straight at us!

I charged straight at the lion and leapt onto it. I dug my sharp talons deeply into the back of the mad lion. He tried to roll over and knock me off him but he was unsuccessful. He finally fell to the ground and I was so shattered I just lay there in the grass. My brothers came over to help me but I was knocked out. They dragged me back to the den and tried to wake me. They tried and tried but finally they went to sleep.

***

The next morning, when I was up and fine again, they told me what had happened. Suddenly I heard antelopes crying out. We dashed outside and we couldn't believe our eyes. There was another Coalition made up of four cheetahs. We sprinted over to them and showed them our den. They said if we wanted to we could join them. Then they came into our den because it was getting late. We all slept and I dreamt about the marvellous adventures we would have.

About the author

Jack Forshew was born and lives in Guildford, Surrey. He lives with his mum, his fourteen-year-old sister, Lisey, his pet beagle, Indie, and Charlie the rabbit. Jack loves nothing more than playing the drums, gaming, programming and making his own games, cricket, music and the odd game of Monopoly, going to waterparks and eating sausages!

The Little African Elephant Calf

Tristan Hartwell

My name is Banda and I am a south-east African elephant calf. I live in a herd of cows (females) and the bulls (males) who have reached puberty and live together on the plain. I am a herbivore like all of the other elephants and my favourite food is red berries. Asian elephants are different from African elephants because they have different shaped heads, tusks and ears.

A few days ago, when the hot African sun was burning against my thick grey back, I was playing at the waterhole. My friends and I were splashing our trunks and our muscular feet, having a fabulous time, when I could hear a faint noise getting closer by the second. It sounded like lions because of their glorious roaring. Everybody had run away by the time the lions arrived but I was concentrating on getting a magnificent red berry hanging off a tree.

When I realised that there were eight lions surrounding me, I started to back into the waterhole hoping they couldn't swim. I trumpeted as loudly as possible, thinking that my friends would come to rescue me. At this point I was really scared that the lions would eat me for dinner, with the shining African sun glimmering off their beautiful golden backs.

Mum, who is the matriarch in our herd, which is the head of the herd and the biggest, heaviest and the most powerful elephant in the herd, arrived in a rush and immediately scared four lions away. I could not believe it was really her. Then she trumpeted and got me under her belly, scared two more lions away and trotted to the rest of the herd.

Unfortunately, I fell and the two lions that remained closed in on me. Mum once again charged back to get me but when she got there, there was a lion grabbing onto her leg. She looked helpless. I wished I didn't have to see her like that. It looked horrible.

After that I could hear a quiet noise getting louder and louder. It was the other bulls that had reached puberty. They must have heard my trumpeting and stampeded all the way to save me. I was delighted to see them again – even my uncle was there. Then I could see my dad. He was determined to save me from those savage lions when he saw that our lives were at risk.

The bulls first charged towards the lions, like the lions had red all over them. The bulls were not stopping until they shoved the lions into the nearby waterhole. Once they had done it they said hello to all of their wives and children until they had to go.

I felt so pleased that I was back with the herd and not about to be eaten by lions. Eventually Mum's leg healed up and she was OK.

***

I learnt that I should always run away when lions appear, even if it involves not getting a red berry hanging from a tree, because my desire for berries nearly killed me.

About the author

Tristan Hartwell is ten years old and lives with his parents in Surrey. He doesn't have any brothers or sisters but does have a large pond in the garden with lots of fish! He loves sport, especially playing tennis and cricket. Ever since he went on holiday to India, he's enjoyed writing stories about elephants and tigers and his favourite book is *Tiger Adventure* by Willard Price.

It's a Rat's Life

Teddy Jenkins

People often misunderstand us rats. They tend to think we are dirty, unhygienic and dangerous. We're associated with rubbish and disease, and I've even heard of witches using our tails in their spells. Ouch!

The truth is that we are a very friendly group. We love nothing more than snuggling up together during the daytime and then scampering around at night, searching for food or digging new tunnels to run through. I come from a large family that lives at the end of a garden of a large white house near the city. I have something like 300 brothers and sisters and I couldn't even begin to tell you how many aunts, uncles, cousins, nieces and nephews I have.

I think we're actually very clean animals. Sometimes we get sick, but my dad says it's because you have to watch out for food in plastic boxes and my mate, Dave, once got caught in a metal cage. Luckily for Dave the cage was rusted so we all managed to gnaw through the corner and rescue him.

***

In the big white house there is a cat called Malcolm. Malcolm used to be really frightening and would jump out from the foliage pinning down whichever one of us he could catch. Luckily for us Malcolm says he prefers cat biscuits to eat, and he's stopped taking us indoors. A few years ago Malcolm was really upset when he took one of us indoors to show his owner. Malcolm got really confused when the owner started shouting at him. He couldn't understand it because they used to buy him stuffed toys that looked like us, and he thought they'd like to meet the real thing.

***

We're just happy living in our own world – sleeping, eating and digging. We try to avoid other animals, especially humans. Humans confuse me. Sometimes they come and dig where we live or get mad when we eat the food they leave out for us. Why would they do that? My dad says that they don't like us because years ago we spread a disease that nearly killed them all. Turns out it wasn't us but one of the lice that sometimes make us itch.

***

The animals we really worry about though are the owls. The owls are these really big birds that just seem to appear out of nowhere. Only last week one of my cousins was just sitting there, having a scratch and then – whoosh – he was gone. You have to stay really quiet and really still when you are out in the open. My trick is to always stick to the edge of the path or stay under something because they come from above and it's really hard to look up without stopping. The only danger is of running into a cat, but Malcolm is my friend and he tends to keep other cats off his territory.

***

I'm just about to become a dad for the thirty-second time. My girlfriend usually has about six babies each time, but last time we had seven babies. They grow up really fast so it's nice to have little ones every year. The only downside is that we have to dig more tunnels but that's alright for me because I love digging.

Next time you see one of us, just remember we're just trying to survive and get along. If you avoid us, we'll avoid you.

About the author

Teddy Jenkins was born in Guildford and has attended Cranmore Prep since the age of three. He has always enjoyed reading and has a fondness for his numerous pet animals, with Carson, the Golden Retriever, taking pride of place. Malcom, the family's ginger moggy, makes a cameo appearance in Ted's short story about rats and he has recently attended a talk on owls that also features in the plot. Teddy hopes to write more stories in the future and this is surely the first of many publications.

🐾 Paws for Thought Discussion Point

I really liked to read a positive story about one of the creatures so many people dislike! What do you think about rats? Do you think it's true what they say? That we're never more than six feet from a rat?

Courage
Emma McCarthy

Chapter 1
Who's that?

Long ago there lived a deer named Ella. Ella lived in a wood with her family. She was scared of everything. She was even scared of finding friends. Ella hated it when her brothers teased her because she was so scared. One day after her brothers teased her, Ella set off to find courage. As she walked along the path she saw something behind a big oak tree.

"Who is there?" Ella said, frightened.

Suddenly something like a kind of snout slowly came out from behind the big oak tree and vanished again. Ella really wanted to know who it was but she was too scared to go to the tree.

Chapter 2
First friendship

Suddenly a trembling wolf came out from behind the big oak tree, his tail wagging. Ella could hear his teeth trembling. Ella wanted to know who he or she was. So she took everything that was in her and asked, trembling,

"What are you called?"

The wolf slowly said, "I'm called Lily. Who are you?"

"I'm Ella, and I'm always scared."

"Well that's funny. I'm also always scared."

The two animals came closer to each other. When they were close together they stopped and sat down. Ella asked Lily why she was always scared. They started talking about why they were scared.

"Perhaps we have the same problem," said Ella. "I would like to carry on walking – would you like to join me?"

They walked on until they came to Crile Lake. It got dark, so they made themselves comfortable and went to sleep.

Chapter 3
A net!

Next morning Lily woke up first and went down to Crile Lake to drink. Ella also woke up and drank at the lake. They didn't talk much but they felt friendly. They decided to walk further down the lake. After two hours they stopped to drink again. Suddenly they heard quiet footsteps so they hid. They knew no person would go into the wood because of the wild animals. They also knew that the hunter would go into the wood to kill wild animals. When the hunter was close enough to see them, they saw that he had a net with him.

Chapter 4
Courage

Quickly they jumped behind a big bush. Then they remembered that they wanted to find courage. Lily said,

"Didn't we want to find courage?"

"Yes," said Ella. "So why don't we try to scare him away?"

"I'm a bit scared," said Lily. "When I count to three... One, two, three!" Together the wolf and the deer jumped on the hunter. Lily bit through his net. The hunter was so surprised and scared that he ran off back to town.

***

Ella and Lily were so happy that they had found courage.

About the author

Emma McCarthy was born in Berlin (Germany) and is still living there with her parents and her seven-year-old sister. She is nine years old (almost ten), loves playing the piano and has recently started hockey. She goes to the Nelson-Mandela-International School in Berlin where she wrote the story within her English class lessons encouraged and supported by her English teacher. This has made her realise how much she enjoys writing and she has carried on with more stories.

The Lethal Royal Bengal Tiger
Vivek Nair

The colossal Royal Bengal tiger prowled through the long grass of the humid Sundarbans Forest. Its strong striped body swayed from side to side. The fiery orange fur with elegant black stripes stood out in contrast to the lush green surroundings. The majestic creature's immense heavy paws with deadly sharp claws crushed the ground underneath as it joyfully ate the helpless buffalo it had just killed. The tiger's foray away from its natural habitat deep within the mangrove forest had paid rich dividends. This was the first sumptuous meal the famished tiger had eaten in days. He tore ravenously into the carcass of the slaughtered animal, blissfully unaware that he was being watched.

***

Over the past few years, life had been slowly changing around home for the group of tigers. A series of floods, hurricanes and storms had changed the landscape of their habitat. Trees had fallen, the smaller animals had disappeared and food was scarce, so the tigers spread out in different directions in search of sustenance.

Here, close to the riverbank, things were different. The air was filled with delicious scents and aromas. There were always a variety of faint sounds that made the tiger feel both excited and nervous. Alligators, monkeys, snakes and other predators like leopards were nowhere to be seen.

Instead the plains on either side of the river were spotted with docile grazing animals. Satiated, the tiger left the carcass and retreated from the riverbank to the relative safety and comfort of the thick foliage of the forest. Unknown to the beast, it had been spotted by the villagers.

***

A day or two passed by before the pangs of hunger returned and the tiger instinctively headed for the riverbank. Under the cover of darkness, he felt more secure. Strangely the riverbank was quiet and empty. There were no grazing cattle or easy prey to ambush. The tiger realised that he would have to venture further afield, following the strange smells and distant noises. Soon the tiger stealthily reached the outskirts of the village. As he edged closer, he was hoping to pounce on an unsuspecting animal. To his utter dismay he realised that the cattle had been put away from the edge of the village behind a wooden fence.

Hungrily, the starving tiger circled the village. His eyes glowed brightly in the moonlight. A few stray dogs started to growl and snarl. They soon disappeared as soon as he stepped out from the shadows. The growls quickly turned into whimpers but the commotion was enough to cause some of the villagers to stir from their slumber. It was a warm but humid tropical night. There were several villagers sleeping outdoors on small cots because of the hot weather. Some of them woke up but others remained still. The big cat froze in his tracks wishing he would not be noticed. Unfortunately, his eyes shone brightly out of the darkness. There was a flurry of activity amongst the villagers and he knew that he had been seen. His hunger, however, clouded his initial response to flee. The tiger pounced on the nearest cot and sunk his enormous sharp teeth into its occupant and dragged the frail old lady like a rag doll into the darkness.

Little did the tiger realise that he had crossed a certain line. He had turned from being a fearsome but respected carnivore, to a merciless man-eater. Word about the tiger attack soon spread to the other villages. The villagers soon found out that there had been more tiger attacks in the nearby villages as well. They were absolutely furious, so they planned to kill every tiger that came near them.

When the hungry tiger returned to the village for another ambush, the villagers were ready and a trap had been set. As the tiger crept into the village, towards the goat tied to a tree, he found it to be eerily quiet. The tiger turned quickly to run but it was too late. Hundreds of humans armed with sticks, stones and lit torches descended on the majestic creature. The endangered species of Royal Bengal tigers were one step closer to extinction.

Royal Bengal Tiger *by Vivek Nair*

About the author/artist

Vivek Nair is a ten-year-old cricket fanatic. He lives in Northwood, Middlesex with his annoying yet loveable, seven-year-old brother and exasperated parents.

He enjoys tennis, karate and wrestling with his brother. He is currently going to St Martin's School in Northwood and is looking forward to his transition to secondary school at Queen Elizabeth School for Boys, Barnet. He enjoys singing, playing the violin and piano. This was his second foray into competitive writing. The first was when he was shortlisted for the BBC 500 words competition.

🐾 Paws for Thought Discussion Point

We probably receive more stories about tigers than anything else and I think we all agree they are beautiful creatures. But in 2014 there are estimated to be less than 3000 tigers left in the wild. The main threats to wild tigers include: habitat loss and fragmentation due to mining, logging, farming and human settlement; depletion of their prey; conflict with humans; and poaching for their skins and other parts and products.

Save Wild Tigers is a global initiative set up in 2010 by Simon Clinton which, working in conjunction with the Born Free Foundation and the Environmental Investigation Agency, aims to provide a unified, focused and co-ordinated global programme of tiger conservation initiatives.

The mission of *Save Wild Tigers* is to provide urgent and ongoing targeted support for tiger conservation in a bid to eradicate the increasing threat of extinction that wild tigers face. Urgent action needs to be taken if Asia's most extraordinary and iconic animal is to be saved from extinction.

Please visit their website *www.savewildtigers.org* for more information.

Years 7 and 8

A note from our judge, Sally Spedding

Sally Spedding was born in Wales and is the acclaimed author of seven crime chillers, *How To Write a Chiller Thriller* and a short story collection, *Strangers Waiting*. She is also a published, award-winning poet who loves the Pyrenees, singing and horses.

Find out more about her by visiting:
www.sallyspedding.com

This is what she said about the stories:

"I found the standard of writing amazing for eleven to thirteen-year-olds and had to re-read several times to decide on the winners. I was looking for engagement with the animal characters and also those with some psychological depth. A really hard job! But so enjoyable.

I chose Maia Freeman's Howl to Save a Life as my winner because it has a great opening and drama a-plenty. The young wolf made a change from those more familiar animals. Pathos too, and a strong narrative drive.

My second place, Saving Atiya by Vienna Cooper, is a terrific story of a young cow elephant, and Mike, the ranger. I was there every step of the way. Visual and moving.

I also chose to highly commend A Monkey's Tale by Alex Cumming as I liked the first-person point of view, and the drama swept me along to a great ending. Again, a more unusual animal was featured."

Winning Story: Years 7 and 8

Howl to Save a Life
Maia Freeman

Rain hammered down from the ominous, marble-grey sky like thousands of miniature knives, drumming through the soaked canopy of leaves and seeping into the sodden earth below. A gentle wind tore through the forest, soft yet deceptive with its freezing undertones. No creature would be desperate or insane enough to venture from their dens in this weather. Yet the trembling howl of a young wolf floated through the trees, barely loud enough to be audible over the deafening roar of the wind and rain. The small wolf howled once more, its voice shaking with desperation. Blue was the smallest of his litter; smoky, mottled grey in colour, with cloudy blue eyes that gave him his name. He was also the weakest, and when his den collapsed, killing his mother and every last one of his siblings, he was shocked beyond measure to find himself alive. However, he expected that he too would die soon – not even the strongest, bravest wolf could survive in conditions such as these with no food and no shelter. The pup whimpered softly before crawling towards a swaying tree and curling up under it, his tiny frame shaking violently.

***

Far away, tucked away in her warm, dry den near the base of a towering mountain, Sky heard the feeble, panicked cries of a wolf, stranded and alone. She pricked her russet-red ears eagerly as she strained to make out more of this stranger. Sky was only young, but had a passion for adventure, even if it put her in great danger. Taking a final, fleeting glance at her mother, who was sleeping peacefully, she took a deep breath and slipped quietly into the torrent of rain and wind.

***

Blue could feel the warmth slowly ebbing from his body, his will to live fading with each torturous moment that passed. Even taking a breath was painful; it would be much easier just to stop moving, just to close his eyes and give in to the blackness that resided at the edge of his vision. He was soaked to the bone; every fibre in his body was freezing and exhausted. He smiled as he looked up and saw the flickering shapes of his mother and siblings, beckoning to him and begging him to join them in the otherworld. Sighing deeply, he relented and allowed his mind to be dragged away.

***

Sky was sure that this was a bad idea. She had the strange wolf's scent and was convinced he was about her age and in ill-condition, but she just couldn't find the cursed thing. However, Sky suspected it had something to do with the fact that the rain seemed to be washing any traces of him away... almost as if he'd left this world altogether. Sky remained positive, determined to prove to her litter-mates that she was the bravest and most skilled wolf out of them all. She too was utterly wet, her usually light red pelt darkened considerably from the rain. Just as she was finally about to give up and turn back, miserable and drenched, she stumbled across the lifeless body of a mottled grey wolf.

***

Blue could feel his mind slipping away from his body, soaring into the storm clouds as he laughed and danced with his mother and siblings. However, he felt a tugging at his heart, a feeling that came from his physical body; back down in the mortal world. He didn't want to go back there, where he was freezing and starving and exhausted; he wanted to be with his family, warm and safe. However, the tugging grew stronger, and he realised he was returning to his physical body; with one last howl of mourning, he opened his grey-blue eyes and felt with a sudden awareness the rain and wind freezing his aching body. He looked up wearily, wondering who had awoken him, and found himself gazing into the most beautiful, multi-toned amber eyes. They were filled with concern and apprehension, and belonged to a rain-soaked young female who appeared to be around his age. She smiled shyly down at him, and from that moment on, Blue knew everything was going to be alright.

***

The twittering of birds and the gentle rustle of leaves as they swayed in the gentle breeze was the only sound that filled the valley. It was springtime, and the scent of blossoms and dewy grass floated like a bird throughout the forest. Nestled safely in a small cave lay two wolves, their long bodies intertwined. One was a female, her soft, russet-red pelt dotted with patches of grey; the larger wolf was a male, his mottled grey coat highlighted with patches of white. Both were old and tired, their bones aching and their heads filled with so many memories, but the sparkle in their eyes was evident as they gazed at one another. Curled up in the soft fur of the female's underbelly were five small pups, each sleeping peacefully as their parents made as little noise as possible. Sky smiled up at Blue, and Blue finally realised that he had been right not to slip away to the otherworld – after all, there was so much worth living for.

Wolf *by Nicole Radtke*

About the author

Maia Freeman is a twelve-year-old girl who lives in Plymouth with her parents and two siblings, Hal and Edie. She was inspired to write her short story after learning more about wolves and how they are hunted for sport.

About the artist

Nicole's love of animals started at a young age and hasn't diminished since. She has two rescue cats at home and wouldn't mind a few more pets. She and her mum have adopted a snow leopard with the WWF. The best part, though, are real animal encounters. So far Nicole has cuddled koalas, fed lemurs, watched dolphins and seals in the wild, and held a baby saltwater croc. She has been stung by jellyfish and bitten by an eel.

Runner-up

Saving Atiya
Vienna Cooper

The bronze, barren grasses of the African Savannah stretched for miles, desperate for the rainy season. Lions slid among the foliage, fearsome predators taking down all the migrating animals as a final feast before they left for the sweeter grasses.

The resident elephant herd was staying in their territory, feeding off the trees. They were too powerful opponents for the lions, who preferred easier pickings. A baby elephant, like their recent birth, Atiya, would be a perfect opportunity, but the herd was large and invincible, a close-knit family similar to humans.

Mike smiled from under his binoculars. He lived in a ranch near the Savannah; this part of the wild was protected from human threat and it was his duty to apprehend any poachers or intruders. He loved waking to the African birds chattering in the trees, the thick blanket of heat in the air, the crickets chirping, the lions roaring to announce the start of a new day. It was pure bliss for him. He had been studying the elephant family for a while, especially Bea and her child. He had named Bea's baby Atiya after an African word that meant gift. He felt it an honour to live near them, and be able to watch the family from his balcony every day. He was part of the wild. Turning away and closing the doors, he slept happily… until he was awoken by the sound of a roaring metal monster… a jeep… speeding into the Savannah.

***

The hunters were pleased with their current bounty – a pile of soft leopard skins, and were preparing to leave. That was when they saw the elephants, looming massively against the dusky sky. The elephants were not the targets, but their tusks. The raw ivory would be prized, merely a large, easy profit for the poachers.

Little Atiya was snuggled against Bea, preparing to sleep, when the hunters rolled up. Immediately she felt the atmosphere shift to one of panic. Her family had always warned her about the most selfish, thoughtless, dangerous species of all. Man. Every Man, except the strange friendly one who lived in the nearby ranch, was to be avoided. Suddenly there was a ripple of loud bangs. Atiya watched in horror as her family started falling. She didn't look back. She vanished into the distance, just as Bea was shot…

***

Mike stumbled out of his house, but the only vehicle he owned, except a pair of legs, was a battered old bicycle. Cursing the poachers, he sighed helplessly. As a cacophony of gunshots went off in the distance, all Mike could do was fall to the ground in despair, as his precious elephant family were killed for ivory. He buried his head in his hands. It wasn't fair… just not fair.

***

Horrible images flashed through Atiya's head. She was so young, naïve to the world, and the harsh reality was almost too much for her to bear. She sunk to the ground as rain began to lash the world. Meanwhile, Mike was struggling through the storm, searching for hope. All he could think of was Bea and her innocent calf. His heart burned with grief and injustice. He wanted to hurt the poachers as they had hurt the animals, make them feel the pain he did. He wanted them to feel the way the elephants had when their family was killed. His stomach disappeared as he found the jeep's tracks, washing away into the mud. Some trees were splintered; a single bullet lay on the ground, smeared with blood. His stomach came back, feeling heavy, as though it was a balloon full of stones.

Most of the herd was dead. Their tusks had been hacked off brutally, their bodies dripping with rain. He began sobbing as he saw Bea's body, no sign of her baby... suddenly, he heard a pitiful noise. There was a large lump, lying under a tree, limp and weak... Atiya. Mike felt both relief and despair, how could he help the baby without her mother? Scooping her up into his arms, straining every muscle to lift the half-ton baby, he took Atiya into the safety of his home. The elephant was terrified, after she had experienced the poachers, she was traumatised, wary of all men. Somehow, though, she trusted Mike. He smelt familiar, of the musky tropical Savannah and the warm aroma of elephants. She fell fast asleep as he wrapped a soft blanket around her.

"Little Atiya," he muttered. "I'll take care of you. I promise."

***

A few months later Atiya was completely recovered. Sometimes she still woke up screaming with nightmares, like a human child, but Mike's presence soon comforted her. Meanwhile, Mike himself had seen another elephant herd, whose matriarch, Elsa, had an elder daughter. Now that Atiya was finally weaned off the milk substitute he had purchased especially for her, it was time to introduce Atiya back into the wild.

***

The grasslands were familiar to Atiya, the scent of her old family and her mother lingering in the air. She felt a pang for her old life, but regarded Mike as her herd now. She had no clue that she was about to transfer to a whole new life once again. The new herd were like giants, she had forgotten how elephants like her looked, compared to her puny friend Mike. They stared at her, the newbie, with inquisitive eyes. Elsa marched forward, a gentle giant, stretching her trunk towards Atiya. Atiya rolled around playfully, kicking out towards Elsa. Elsa lowered her face and stroked the baby, before looking at Mike meaningfully. Atiya had been accepted. His eyes filled with tears at the sight. He hoped Atiya would inherit the position of matriarch after her new adoptive mother. He patted her rump and prepared to leave, but as he began to walk, Atiya let out a hurt squeal. She circled him with her soft leathery trunk, refusing to let go. He patted her head, looking into her melting eyes.

"Grow up good and strong," he told her.

She gurgled, almost in agreement, before finally letting go and following her new family.

***

A few years later, Mike was married. He had decided to take retirement from the African Savannah, and take a safer job like his wife wanted. It was time to head back home, to England. It was like a foreign land after being in such an exotic country for two decades. He looked over the land one last time and something by the gleaming sapphire waterhole caught his eye; a herd of elephants driving a hungry pride of lions away. The largest female of the herd was leading the attack. Mike let out a cry, to his wife, to see the wonder. The lead elephant heard his cry, and whipped around. She would recognise that voice from anywhere, a deep, warm rumble, full of compassion and kindness, not tainted with the harshness the poachers' voices had had. Mike recognised her too, her brown eyes, her wrinkled skin, everything.

It was Atiya. And standing by her side, trunks entwined, were two young calves. They were miniature replicas of Atiya herself, clearly her offspring. Joyously, Mike looked down at his own new-borns, small twins, a girl and a boy. He wondered vaguely if Atiya and his wife may have given birth on the same day. He decided, although he had told himself never to interfere with Atiya's life in the wild, he would go and say goodbye. He darted down the steps and through the grass, not paying any attention. He ran as fast as his achy legs would take him. As he neared the waterhole, a vulture spooked him and he lost his balance. He toppled to the ground and into the waterhole. He tried to grab hold of a nearby log, but when he did, the log rose to the surface, revealing a yellow eye and rows of blade-like teeth... a crocodile! He desperately thrashed trying to swim away, but the crocodile was gliding smoothly closer, undeterred.

As Mike's leg tangled in weed, he closed his eyes and waited for the killer bite. Suddenly, he felt the sensation of a tight rope squeezing his middle. It was Atiya, lifting him out of the water. She used all her strength, returning the favour from years ago, saving Mike's life. She lowered him onto the bank. The other elephants surrounded him, recognising him as Atiya's old foster-father. "Thank you," he whispered, stroking her face. She blinked at him, cradling him lovingly with her trunk. A final goodbye.

***

As Mike got home, his wife scolded him playfully, looking at his wet clothes and the brown Savannah grass clinging to him. "Where have you been?" she asked, mystified.

"I was meeting someone," he said, deciding to spare her the shocking details of his fortunate escape from the crocodile.

"Who?"

He hesitated before replying. "An old friend."

And, just at that moment, the sound of an elephant rumbled in the distance.

About the author

Vienna Cooper is thirteen and lives in Sussex with her parents. She enjoys reading, writing, acting and playing and listening to music, especially rock and metal music. She would love to be an author or actress. She strongly believes in animal rights and thinks that wild animals should be left to be wild.

Highly Commended

A Monkey's Tale

Alex Cumming

A screeching roar echoed through the jungle, making leaves to shiver and branches to crash to the Brazilian wet forest floor.

I leapt through the trees followed by sixteen others, athletically swinging from tree to tree, my lean body like a spring. We all knew what made that sound. My heart beat like a hammer with every jump, my lungs were on fire, but I had to lead the group to safety. All I could see in front of me was a mass of green, but I dove through it, cutting through the vines like a sharp knife, showers of plants exploding behind me.

Suddenly another sound could be heard, this time a faint whisper behind us. We must be gaining distance. With a loud cheer, the group began screeching and shouting, their mouths gaping open and their eyes bright with hope, but all of a sudden, as I looked back towards my friends, a branch wrapped around my leg, twisting and curling like a whip. I was thrown off the tree, tail flailing, hoping that it could grab a hold on the way down. But it didn't. I was sent headfirst into the mud with a loud crash and felt the oozing liquid begin to cover me, spreading over my glistening fur, trapping me. I tried many times to roll around, but my foot was twisted and deformed.

Beginning to lose hope, I opened my huge mouth as wide as I could and sent a deafening howl through the jungle, knowing that my group would be able to hear the call from miles away.

After an agonising wait, the leaves began to ruffle around me, and I desperately lifted myself up, but fell almost immediately. The pain was unbearable. At least my group had come back for me though. They could protect me... my thoughts were interrupted by a loud snap of a twig; jerking my head towards the bushes I saw a pair of gleaming red eyes, a smooth, small, jet black nose and a snarling, dribbling grin. Frantically, I pushed away with my arms, but it was no use. The jaguar advanced, creeping slowly through the mass of plants, revealing smoke-like patches of spots and fiery, muscular skin. I began to shiver and screech hysterically until my massive throat was burning with agony. My bones shivered and rattled in my body, and I waited for my fatal peril.

Suddenly siren-like noises filled the jungle and brown blurs streaked through the canopies, beating their chests and creating a drum-like rhythm. They rapidly slid down the branches and surrounded me, still yelling. The jaguar began to advance and a few of the smaller creatures stepped back, scared of the beast's long jagged teeth. I thought it was going to attack, but then, all of a sudden, it stepped back slowly and retreated into the dense forest. The animals continued to howl, as if they would never stop. We lived up to our name. We were the Howler Monkeys.

About the author

Alex Cumming is a thirteen-year-old boy who lives with his dad, mum and younger brother in Hertfordshire. He developed his English skills at St Martin's school, where he was inspired to write by the brilliant English department there. He loves D.T, playing on his Xbox and sharing jokes with his school friends. Alex likes to read teen fiction books like *The Hunger Games* and *The Enemy* but also loves fantasy stories like *Harry Potter* and *Percy Jackson*.

Soot

Henry Gadsdon

Soot stood proud and tall wearing his smooth, sleek, soot-black feathers like a dinner jacket.

The vast Antarctic Desert stood to the left of him and the even bigger Southern Ocean stood to his right. All the other emperor penguins were starting to line up for a dive. Soot hesitated for a millisecond, realising that he was standing away from the crowd, and then he too joined the line. Soot dived gracefully into the pristine water without a splash. Soot flew through the crystal clear water and his amber beak closed around a fish. Using the last of his air, Soot broke the surface of the ocean, took a deep breath and dived back through the pristine water. This time Soot's worst fear came true as a leopard seal darted out from the ice flows at the speed of light. Soot immediately performed a backflip and swam back the way he had come – but the seal gave chase as fast as a leopard!

Turning back, Soot caught sight of the leopard seal and accelerated like a car joining a motorway to get away from his predator. The black spotted creature saw its prey getting further away from it. As quick as a gunshot the leopard seal sped up to catch Soot. Soot, who was out of breath, swam up to the surface of the Southern Ocean, leaped out of the water in an arc and then dived back into the uncontaminated water.

The leopard seal followed Soot to the surface, when he could have easily got his meal by waiting at the bottom of Soot's arc, and jumped, following Soot all the way, determined to get his meal. Soot looked back and saw the leopard seal was even closer behind him; in fact he was just behind him! Just as the jaws behind him were about to snap shut around Soot's feet, Soot dived and the leopard seal received a mouthful of salt water. Soot ascended and leaped out of the water onto the Antarctic Desert, a long way from his colony. He looked out to sea and saw the leopard seal, deprived of a meal, was swimming under one of the many icebergs that littered the Southern Ocean. Suddenly Soot heard a cry from above his head and instantly looked up! There he saw a lost Australian sea eagle diving towards him as if he were breaking the one hundred metres world record. Soot lay on his snow white belly and started to toboggan down the icy hill away from the ferocious sea eagle, towards his colony.

Soot was lost and all he knew was to get away from the sea eagle. The eagle dived but Soot was too quick for it and it landed face first in the snow. Paralysed for a second, the eagle took off again with hatred glaring in its eyes. Knowing that it would come after him Soot developed a plan. Soot knew that if he positioned himself in such a way that he could jump out the way, the eagle would dive straight into the Southern Ocean. Soot performed this action beautifully and knowing that both the seal and eagle could no longer harm him, he started to trudge back to his colony.

About the author

Henry Gadsdon is an eleven-year old boy who lives with his mum, dad and (sometimes annoying) brother. He loves to play Minecraft to create buildings or just survive. When he grows up he would like to be an actor. Henry loves animals and has two pet cats: James and Galileo. His favourite animal is the penguin. He would like to thank his English teacher Mrs Wood for helping him create this story.

Soot is dedicated to Newton one of his pet cats who sadly passed away in 2013. He was much loved and is much missed.

The Creature and the Foal

Honey Hilton

The stallion looked back at his pursuer. Plainly it was some dog-type creature, tearing madly through the undergrowth in search of its prey.

It was hard to recall how the chase started; it was so sudden! One minute he was with his herd, on the edge of the forest, the next, everyone had scattered because this ferocious ball of fur and teeth had hurled itself at them. However, the stallion discovered that one of his heavily pregnant mares was cantering beside him, the terrified look in her eyes making it clear that she was too stressed out to be good for her. He was fresh and ready to run for miles, whereas the mare wasn't. Not by a long shot.

He knew. She knew. She wouldn't make it. Breathing heavily, she fumbled through the ever-growing mass of brambles, more for her foal than for herself. The stallion could just distinguish her shape, stumbling around and struggling to keep up. He made his way towards her. She couldn't make it – could she?

As she slowed to a dead stop, the stallion wheeled around to meet the snarling creature. It was growling at the mare… ready to pounce. It was as if she had given up all her hope of surviving. All the energy she had put into escaping was gone – she suddenly started to tremble and collapsed on the ferny ground in exhaustion. Lashing out at the creature, the stallion whinnied to reassure the mare, before the creature turned on him and started to give chase again.

There was a small river, winding like a ribbon through the heart of the forest. Ripples spread across its surface and birds twittered happily to each other in the treetops overhead. Immediately the tranquillity of this area was disturbed by the chase; everything was chaos. There were animals desperately trying to get out of the way, thrashing, biting, and doing whatever it would take. Amongst all this, the stallion was kicking the creature into the water. But he slipped. He galloped back out of the river, the creature hot on his heels.

***

Meanwhile, floundering about, the mare leant on an old, dead oak tree. Creak! Snap. The stallion darted away just in time to avoid the falling branch, but the creature was not so lucky. He whinnied joyfully to the mare. But she didn't reply. Her burden was gone. Her foal had been born.

Around half an hour later, the young colt was tottering about on his gangly legs. His mother nuzzled him gently, and her big, brown eyes were filled with happiness. His sire looked on in pride at his son, and they settled down as the pale red sky slowly turned into a blanket of stars above them.

***

… Ten years later …

He scanned his eyes over the herd, making sure they were safe. What he didn't know was that this was the place where his father's herd was first attacked by the creature. Some never came back, but others did, searching for him and his mother. His mother. She hadn't survived the long trek back, and his father had from then on protected him. No one had ever seen any other creatures like the one they had faced, either. Good.

About the author

Honey Hilton lives on a small beef cattle farm in Kent with her grandparents, and attends Sir Roger Manwood's Grammar School in Sandwich. Her favourite animals are cows, and one of her best friends is a cow called Chocolate! There are a lot of different animals on the farm, including rare breed sheep, cows, horses, ducks, geese, chickens, two dogs, two guinea-pigs and a cat. When she's older she would like to be a journalist, and travel around the world. She would most like to travel to Asia (India, China, Thailand), to learn all about the customs and traditions... and, of course, because of the spicy foods!

Zebra *by Morgan Joy Ashby (cover artist)*

🐾 Paws for Thought Discussion Point

What do you know about how zebras are related to horses? See what you can find out. Why do you think zebras have stripes and horses don't?

A Mud Bath

Tayin Lakhani

A light breeze blew swiftly through the savannah. The sun rose higher in the sky and an orchestra of sound could be heard from all around the dusty plains. Animals of all kinds could be heard.

Coated in a sheet of red mud, a Warthog trotted over to a spring. The Warthog dipped his snout to take a sip of the clear blue water. Suddenly a Gazelle shot past the Warthog. The Warthog gingerly lifted his head up and scanned his surroundings; he cocked his head from side to side. A wall of dust rose in the distance. Moving faster and faster. Getting closer and closer. Eventually a herd of Gazelles stampeded past the Warthog, sending it running for his life. The Warthog landed with a loud splash in the spring it was about to drink from. He got back on his feet, looking and listening for the sound of a predator. A loud snarl-like roar echoed around the savannah. The Warthog spotted a burrow in the distance and scurried towards it. The Warthog was a smoky grey and could easily be seen all through the yellow dusty savannah. He was only a few steps away from the burrow, but it was too late. A sleek golden Leopard with a scattering of jet black spots emerged into the Warthog's view.

The Leopard quickly moved forward, advancing on the Warthog. The Warthog's instincts kicked in, telling him to run. Despite his small chubby frame he tore through the savannah, only fractionally faster than the Leopard. Crashing through springs and crossing the humid and dusty savannah, the Leopard was hot on the Warthog's heels. Twisting round every bend and every turn, the Leopard followed. The Warthog started to run on the muddier terrain and moved forward smoothly, but behind him the Leopard was skidding around. The Leopard couldn't get a grip on the slick muddy ground. The Warthog started to trot along the mud with a slight spring in his step, and then darted quickly inside a hollow log. Far behind the Warthog, the Leopard was turning back and had given up on chasing the Warthog. The Warthog trotted quickly out of its log and looked around for a spring. Eventually the Warthog found a spring full of sapphire blue water.

It was about noon and the sun was high in the sky. It was blazing hot and the Warthog lay basking in the shallow waters of a spring. The sun gleamed off its two pairs of tusks. All was calm and the wind blew gently, cooling down the Warthog, but still he remained alert; always watching. The Warthog trotted quickly out of the spring, trying not to be seen. Suddenly a golden figure pounced onto the Warthog. With all of its strength, the Warthog threw off his attacker and left it sprawled across the hard dry ground. The Warthog took off, leaving a loud and angry snarl behind. The Leopard had picked itself up off the ground and was already bounding towards the defenceless Warthog. The Warthog ran as fast as it could and managed to stay ahead of the Leopard.

Soon the Warthog heard a soft growl and looked back to see the Leopard lying on the ground panting for air. The Warthog trotted away with a spring in its step and left the Leopard behind. The sun was low in the savannah now and, with his tail pointing up, the Warthog trotted around treading on lush green grass, looking for a burrow. As after the two chases he could not find his own burrow. Orange and red beams of light were cast across the warm land. After a long day's hard work the Warthog settled down in a new burrow he found and rested his weary body, watching the sun disappear from view in the savannah.

About the author

Tayin Lakhani is twelve years old and lives in Pinner. Tayin lives with his mum, dad and his little sister. Being published again in this book is a great achievement for Tayin. Tayin likes art, especially drawing and he loves reading. But these are just some of Tayin's hobbies. Despite not liking cats and dogs, Tayin takes interest in looking at more wild animals. Tayin enjoys reading fantasy books and action adventure books. Two of his favourite authors are Rick Riordan and Robert Muchamore. Tayin also enjoys reading books by Michael Morpurgo because they give Tayin more of a feel for animals.

Tayin attends St Martin's School in Northwood. His favourite subject is Design Technology where he has made many things based on some of the books he has read.

The Elusive *Panthera uncia*
Manas Madan

It was one of the harshest, most severe winters in the awe-inspiring Himalayas.

Cruel blizzards and shrieking squalls beat incessantly at the perpendicular cliffs, so high that they seemed to touch the sky. The landscape was white as ghostly shrouds, justifying why the great mountain range was known as the Abode of Snow.

Looming dangerously was a craggy outcrop; beneath it, the tempest relented to give some relief. In the foggy darkness of a well-protected cave, among the frolicking of her three cubs, the mother arose from her uneasy slumber. Unwrapping her thick tail and stretching her sinewy legs, the desperation of the predicament struck her again.

She reflected, with grimness, the happy memories with her family not so long ago. She had grown up in these parts to become a strong and spirited snow leopard. Her soft silky coat was speckled with dark grey to black rosettes; this served as an excellent camouflage while hunting. Her tail was bushy and paws padded with thick fur. She would never tire of exploration and a sense of adventure. She knew about every crack and crevice, every bush and tree, every village where she would sometimes foray for Bharal sheep.

In one particularly bright and salubrious summer, she met a robust and handsome snow leopard during the mating season, whom she immediately became fond of. His stocky structure was covered with sleek glistening fur and with large eyes as blue as sapphires, and he was the perfect partner she had been looking for.

Together many a day – be it sunny or snowy – they would scale dizzying heights with their powerful, wiry limbs. Chasing each other down the steep mountain slopes and ragged terrain, they dashed like silver bolts of lightning across the breath-taking panorama. They would criss-cross along sheer paths trying to find the source of gushing mountain streams. Hunting for them was a cakewalk – after eating to their hearts' content, they would lie supine on a hill top, basking in the luxuriant sunshine.

They became much happier with the arrival of their three beautiful little cubs – full of mischief and curiosity. The snow leopard growled in despair as she remembered with vividness, the fateful day that would change their lives forever. It was a harsh winter and wild prey was getting scarce. So she and her mate had gone to the nearby village in the middle of the night. Two of the older cubs, whom they were training to hunt, accompanied them. Stealthily, using their hunting senses, smell and impeccable eyesight, they made their way towards a corral. The enclosure housing a few sheep and goats seemed safe. They moved soundlessly – the domestic animals grew uneasy, but could not see the hidden danger. Suddenly, two dark shapes sprang from a height upon the animals. By now, there was great agitation among the animals – the 'baas' and the bleats grew in decibels. The leopards had caught a sheep each and were trying to immobilise and kill them.

Bang!

A sharp shot ricocheted in the still air.

The she-leopard dropped her clutch of the bleating sheep that was now unconscious and looked up. Humans carrying long shining rods rushed in from all directions, forming a semi-circle around the snow leopard. For a moment, she was paralysed with terror and fear. Another shot rang menacingly close. It was a trigger for action. Her partner threw himself in front of the men, forming a protective shield for herself and her two cubs. He growled, keeping them back.

"Quickly, run with the children, go home, don't worry I will be right behind you," her companion reassured her.

"No!"

She wouldn't; after all they had been through. She could not leave him.

"You have to. Save our cubs," he protested. "I love you," he whispered softly.

Tears welled up in her eyes but she knew that she had to escape to save her young ones.

***

A third bang sounded, she fled with her cubs out of harm's way, and she looked back. Even at that distance, she could make out her companion, bravely facing the savage humans. Injuring or even killing a few of them, after a bloody battle the last shot ended it all. She still did not forgive herself for abandoning her mate that dreadful night.

The snow leopard flipped back to the present moment. The thought of the death of her partner, her only companion, was painful and unbearable even now. She recalled the utter loneliness and anguish she went through, and the tormenting rage she felt for the killer. It was only for the sake of her little ones that she summoned up the will and courage to go on.

In this particularly severe winter, wild prey was getting scarce and hunting more demanding. She did venture into the village once in a while, but she knew it was quite dangerous. She had seen that the dwellers in the village had long rods through which fire and smoke came out – strong enough to kill, like it had killed her mate. The cubs were older now; but it would be another few summers before they would be confident to hunt on their own. Hence, she feared for the near future and knew that she had to be strong and alive for their sake.

The big cat pulled herself together, pushing her great loss to the back of her mind. Knowing that she needed to hunt a large animal that would serve as food for her and her cubs for the next week or two, she ventured out of the cave, anxious yet optimistic.

The snow leopard penetrated into the nippy, numbing night, bracing against the roaring winds. Icicles like sparkling crystal decorations hung down from the roof of the cave. Her footprints were engraved into the blanketed ground. Wicked white wonder smothered the land all down to the horizon. Encrusted large rugged rocks trapped as it were in an icy prison; stuck out abruptly, like skeletal fingers ready to grab unsuspecting prey. The snow-clad mountain tips were shrouded with mist. Only the toughest of flora and fauna lived in such adverse conditions. Amid those, the snow leopard was probably one of the toughest and most adept to the terrain.

The snow leopard's coat shimmered with drops of sweat oblivious to the sub-zero temperature, tensed due to the precarious predicament. Covered in thick glossy fur with dark grey rosettes, the fierce cold did not dent her determination. Her nose sniffed at the chilled air for the trace of a possible meal. Her pale green eyes glistened in the austere moonlight.

Using her stocky body and wide paws, she bounded from rock to ridge with ease, single-minded in her urgent movements. Her long thick tail helped her keep her balance on such uncertain rocky terrain.

A scent of prey drifted through the air. The leopard's impeccable eyesight spotted what could be the solution for her worries.

A large *Capra ibex* stood still upon a ledge. Its sleek tanned beard blowing in the wind and tall curved antlers standing proud. Although in rest, it was still alert in case of danger.

The snow leopard crouched on her belly and crept closer and closer to the ibex, stalking as near to the lying ibex as possible. At the spur of the moment, she sprang from a great height and surged into action; the ibex was alerted to the danger and bounded away.

She was soon close in pursuit, sprinting after the fleeing ibex and gradually reducing the distance between them. Her thick furry paws gripped the snow laden crags firm; her body and leg muscles rippled with the amplified power of her sinuous movements.

Weaving through the protruding rocks, twisting and turning sharply, she still exuded rhythmic grace. Adrenalin pumped high with excitement in the snow leopard's body – blood rushed in her veins as she closed in for the kill – steely in her determination not to let her prey escape.

Her claws slashed through the fleshy rump of the ibex. Desperate for survival, the ibex used all its strength and tore away from her, jumping into a mountain stream escaping narrowly from the snow leopard's clutches.

The weak rays of the sun eventually broke through the dense bulging clouds. Maybe there was still a glimmer of hope for her and her cubs. She waited, gazing into the dawning horizon.

About the author

Manas Madan was born in India and now currently lives in Hertfordshire with his parents. He studies in St Martin's School – Northwood. He thinks man's progress has a devastating side effect – depletion of habitats of wild animals. He found it a joy to write this story for which he chose the elusive and mysterious snow leopard after a lot of research. An avid reader and a devoted fan of Steve Backshall's *Deadly 60* and David Attenborough on Nature, Manas likes to dabble in art or tinker in D.T when he's not playing racquet games like tennis, badminton or logic games like chess. Manas is a self-confessed day dreamer and likes to go on adventures and gaze at beautiful landscapes.

He is thrilled to have his first story published. He thanks his English teacher for her support and dedicates this story to his parents.

Black Panther *by Tayin Lakhani*

About the artist

Tayin Lakhani also has a story in the collection – as well as being a talented artist! Read about him after his story.

🐾 Paws for Thought Discussion Point

We seem to receive a lot of stories about the wonderfully elusive snow leopard, also known as the mountain ghost. This beautiful story captures the essence of this majestic wild cat so well. Sadly there are believed to be 4,500 – 7,500 snow leopards left in the wild in 2014. Habitat degradation, mostly through excessive livestock grazing, occurs on a vast scale in areas of snow leopard habitat.

Snow leopards are also highly vulnerable to poaching, and the illegal trade in pelts and bones presents a serious threat. The rising frequency and number of poachers and traders intercepted on their way into China with snow leopard parts, indicates that demand for such products is increasing. Few, if any, protected areas are free of human influence, and even those large enough to encompass a snow leopard's entire home range cannot provide full protection for these big cats. There are programmes intended to try to protect this beautiful creature before it's too late. Find out what you can do too.

I chose to put Tayin's Black Panther drawing after this story as this animal is related to the snow leopard as well as many of the big cats. So can you find out how they're related? What is the Latin name of the black panther? See how it's similar to the snow leopard. What other cat are they like and what different names does the panther have on other continents?

Hope

Ryan Ratnam

Darkness surrounded her. Thrashing her flippers about and wriggling her body, she desperately made her way to the surface. A sense of fear drove her on. She knew she must get out. She knew she was in danger but she didn't know what from. Her pointed, leathery head broke through the sand. Momentarily she was blinded by the sun and she blinked her small beady eyes. She felt dazed as her ears were assaulted with a symphony of sounds for the first time. Kicking free of the remnants of shell from which she had emerged, she scrambled out of the pit and clumsily staggered across the beach. She was followed by more and more animals that looked just like her. They were her many siblings who had hatched from the other soft white eggs which their mother had buried. So many came out, forming a bedraggled line across the golden sand.

The beach was calm, fringed with palm trees gently swaying in the warm breeze. Rhythmically, the waves lapped up to the shore. But all too soon, the serenity was broken by a riot of noise. A multitude of seagulls swooped down from their overhead kingdom, squawking as they descended. They latched on to the baby turtles, picking them off, one by one. The helpless babies were ravenously devoured by the flying monsters. Filled with terror, the remaining turtles stumbled into the sea, swimming fast and furiously. The seagulls could no longer find their prey and retreated back to the sky. The turtles were in their kingdom now, the water. But unbeknown to them, the kingdom was shared.

***

Some months earlier, when the turtles had not yet met the world, danger had threatened them. They were still eggs inside their mother. She was ready to lay her eggs and came at dusk. The sun was setting like a huge orange melting into the sea. She was old and cumbersome and moved slowly. When she arrived, the prime areas of the beach had already been nested on. She was forced to dig her pit near the trees. During the day there would be shade here and her eggs would not be warm enough. They would not incubate and her babies would not grow. This was a bad place to nest but she had no choice. She had to lay and bury her eggs before morning broke. She left knowing she would never see her young hatch.

***

Several days passed and the eggs lay still and silent in their sandy cradle. It was then that they came, the two-legged ones. They carried shovels and buckets. Without mercy or thought they raided the nests throwing sand up everywhere. The eggs were taken away and would never hatch. They would be eaten or used for native medicine. But the two-legged ones had overlooked one nest, the one under the shady trees. And so the little baby turtle and her many siblings had survived their first peril.

***

The surviving baby turtles' fear had now abated. They flapped their flippers vigorously trying to swim but they were still so small, the current carried them along. The aqua blue desert stretched endlessly into the horizon. At first they swam near the surface for fear of the darkness below them. The darkness was foreboding and mysterious, but they were curious. Swimming close together, they ventured deeper. The kingdom of the ocean opened up beneath them. They weaved through darting shoals of fish, some large, some small. The ocean floor was carpeted with verdant green plants and a plethora of colourful corals. This was their home and they felt safe.

They were many months old now. Having fed well on all the ocean had to offer, they had become bigger and stronger. They didn't bob along like small toys carried on the current anymore but were now able to swim where they wanted to. But their peace was broken by the hidden lair that lay in wait for them below the surface, the fishing nets! Without warning they were entangled in the sprawling nets. They struggled frantically, entangling themselves further. The nets cut into their flippers. They must get out or they would drown. Exhausted and filled with hopelessness, the young female turtle stopped struggling, accepting that they were going to die in these nets. These were the contraptions of the two-legged ones. The nets hung down from a large boat. Along with the fish that would be ensnared in the nets, the two-legged ones wanted the turtles for the beautiful brown colours of their shells.

Without warning, from the depths of the darkness, something hit the nets like a missile. It was a shark! His mouth was open wide, baring his jagged, stained teeth. The trapped turtles were easy prey for the shark and they could see from his angry eyes that he was determined to have them. Using his strong muscular body, he rammed into the net which eventually gave way and broke. The young turtles spilled out of the net like air from a punctured balloon. They swam around haphazardly not knowing which way to safety. The young female managed to swim away from the commotion. She turned to see her remaining siblings being devoured by the monstrous predator.

***

Five years had passed and the turtle was now a fully grown majestic female. She glided through the water like a giant albatross soaring through the skies. Her shell was a beautiful mosaic, marbled with hues of amber and gold. Her belly was now heavy with young and she had to find a safe place to nest. She was most probably the only one of her siblings left. One thing was certain; she would never see them again.

The ocean was still and tranquil. She started to make her way closer to land but the sea had other ideas. Something was coming; something which would wipe the earth like never before. It would rip the trees from their roots, the fish would be left to die on the land and she was in the middle of it. The seabed rumbled beneath her. The noise ascended like a thunderous drum. A strong shockwave rippled through the sea and the water trembled. She went to the surface in an attempt to get to the safety of land. She was ever conscious of her belly, heavy with eggs. What she saw before her was black; just black. A colossal wall of black water was crashing towards her. It blocked out the sun and seemed to be as tall as the sky. It was as if Poseidon himself had struck the sea with his massive fist. Desperately she tried to swim away as fast as she could, but she was heavy and slow and the tsunami was faster;

much faster. Crashing down on her like a falling building, the wave dragged her under. She tried to get above the water but she was no match for its power. The wave enveloped her like heavy sheets. Her lungs had already begun to fill with water. One thought kept going through her head; she was going to die. She was spinning around uncontrollably when finally the waves smashed her, like a rag doll, against the rocks just off the shore. She wailed in pain but not for her, for her young.

***

Darkness had fallen and the waters were calm once more. She found herself at the edge of the shore with only the stars for company. Ahead she could see the beach strewn with debris. She dragged her broken body further up the beach. This was a good place to nest but instinct took hold of her and drove her on. Not here, she thought. And then she saw it; a group of palm trees. Their leaves were frayed and their branches broken. Under the shade of trees was not a good place to nest but something told her she must get there. She used every ounce of strength she had and hauled herself towards the trees. The excruciating pain seared through her with every move. Under the trees and using her hind flippers, she dug out her pit. Relief washed over her and she laid her eggs. She knew this had to be the place. She knew this must be the place; the place where her mother had laid her eggs; the place where she had entered the world. With barely any energy left, she covered the pit and made her way back to the ocean. She knew it was quite likely, her eggs would not survive, but maybe, just one, like her, would overcome the odds, and reach the ocean. Maybe her daughter would return to this place to lay her eggs. Her heart filled with hope.

About the author

Ryan Ratnam is a twelve-year-old school boy who lives in Harrow with his parents, sister and two cats, Harry and Hermione. He attends Queen Elizabeth's Grammar School in Barnet. In his spare time Ryan enjoys playing cricket and rugby. He also plays the cello, piano and the drums. His cats usually run for cover whenever he does a drums practice!

Ryan's story was inspired following a visit to a turtle conservation project centre in Sri Lanka, which he visited while on holiday there. At the centre he saw how eggs were collected from the beach, incubated and hatched and finally released back into the ocean. He was able to hold the baby turtles, who were very wriggly! He also saw many injured turtles being cared for at the centre, who would not be able to survive in the wild. The most moving for him was seeing a turtle with only one front flipper who had been injured in the Tsunami of 2004. Ryan hopes to do some volunteering work at the centre at some point in the future.

The Story of a Real Hunter

Thomas Rochussen

The first light that ever entered my eyes was reflected from the giant, golden orbs of my mother's eyes.

I remember the first few moments of my life, in a 'scrape' on top of a mound, with black and white feathers all around me. Now I know that all owlets are black and white, as opposed to the pure white that I am today.

From that moment onwards, the other owlets, my siblings as I now know them to be, always dominated me as I was the runt of the mound. With my parents, life was easy; they brought me food, usually mouse flesh, but sometimes we would feast on something like a squirrel, a bird or even a small fox cub. I ate, they hunted, and so it continued until one day when my parents were hunting, my siblings took things too far by trying to push me off the mound onto deep snow, where an owlet would sink and never get out again. I remember my terror, the feeling that I was never going to see life again, when suddenly one of our parents came out of seemingly nowhere and intervened. From then on, I lived in a different mound, separated from the others by the deep snow where no owlet ventures.

A few moons later I woke up early one dusk to find that both my parents and siblings were missing from the mounds. I looked up into the sky and saw seven shapes soaring above, white against the darkening sky. My siblings were flying, they were actually flying! I tried to take off, but my underdeveloped wings were just pushing air up and down but not creating any lift. The largest of my siblings dived down as he saw me struggling, and was laughing at me with his booming voice reverberating around the valley. My other siblings copied him, and all I did was sit there feeling depressed and useless – the failure.

***

A year later, I was able to fly when our parents took us on a hunt, our first hunt. Having flown into the forest, we flew between the trees but the forest was dense, almost too dense. We were weaving in and out of the trees, seemingly faster and faster and, while my siblings seemed exhilarated, I was getting more and more nervous. My siblings began to taunt me, one of them saying, "Not scared are we, little baby?" He then flew off sniggering.

Thud!

I had been watching him fly off and had not seen the tree ahead of me.

Dawn was breaking. I looked up the vertical slope of the tree trunk… I was lying on my back, on the ground in the forest. Having collected my thoughts, I flew back to the home mound. I was still quite high up, when I heard what they were saying, that I had crashed into a tree and died, and that everyone must forget about me. No compassion, no sadness, just acceptance.

From then onwards I lived far away from them. I so wanted to become bigger than everyone else, stronger and a better hunter. I resorted to living off stolen pieces of meat left at campsites by humans, and occasionally finding injured animals on the ground. I continued flying faster and longer each day, getting stronger and bigger, my wingspan getting broader without my noticing. One day I flew alongside an eagle, and he did not seem as enormous as my parents had described, but almost smaller than I was.

I have still not made my first live hunt – and now, here I am, soaring over the mountains, floating on the breeze, higher than any normal owl flies. I am determined to hunt larger prey, and my determination burns inside of me; my life's goal has to be achieved now.

Then I see a flicker, a tiny movement on the side of the mountain, next to a tree, standing up alert... a marmot. I can visualise its face and am suddenly filled with a sense of strength and power as my speeding body lurches forward and downwards towards it, faster and faster, dropping out of the sky, a white arrow of feathers. I focus only on the marmot.

My talons open.

My pupils widen.

My adrenaline pumps.

My blood flows.

My mind races.

Then my talons crush the soft warm body as I reach my destination. I immediately fly away, my prey dangling below me. Out the corner of my eye I see another sight, a familiar one of the home mound, filled with my siblings.

The kill is limp and heavy as it swings in my talons, but my victory only allows me to think how proud my parents will be of me. I am, at last, a real owl, a real predator, a real hunter.

About the author

Thirteen-year-old Thomas Rochussen is a South African born boy who lives in Surrey. He adores playing, listening to and composing classical music. When he is not playing hockey or doing downhill mountain biking, he researches science topics, particularly physics. When he was younger (and still today) he often watches documentaries by his 'good friend Dave', who turned out to be Sir David Attenborough. He has always been interested in animals – his favourite being the magnificent Snowy Owl who stars in his story of *A Real Hunter*.

An Elephant's Journey

Lakshman Samarakoon

The giant lumbered onwards in a line of enormous beings. Those who could not go on were left to die. The thunderous sound of stamping feet could be heard thousands of miles away. One elephant, who had died in the scorching heat, was already rotting away. Maggots squirmed inside. Yellow pus oozed out of bite marks. Leopards scavenged for any scraps they could find, rotten or fresh. They tore away large chunks of flesh and the trickle of blood formed a pool around the carcass. The vile leopards lapped the red pool of liquid up from the scorched earth. However, the large mammals continued to plod on ahead, fixated on reaching their destination.

There were a few obstacles in the way of the enormous creatures but they had made the same journey many a time in the past. Their dull grey coats were good for camouflage during the night. The hairs sprouted like thorns out of its body. Two white swords protruded straight out, protecting the face and the elongated nose. Suddenly, there was a flash of lightning right next to them and almost immediately afterwards there was a clap of thunder. The giants stampeded in every direction. The bullet like raindrops pelted the helpless creatures.

There was a BANG!!!

Then another.

Guns.

The firing started. Even more animals fell on the rock hard ground. It was a massacre.

***

The next morning, the full extent of the damage was revealed. Corpses of humans, elephants and even other animals were strewn across the ground. The sickening smell of blood filled the air in the area. However, one had survived. The small creature emerged out of the darkness. A baby elephant. All it had known was lost. Its mother and father dead. It was alone. Its legs were trembling but it rose up and carried on.

The infant elephant was vulnerable to all danger, leopards, snakes and even nature itself. It was afraid and worried. Its legs were still shaking. It looked up and saw the heads of trees sheared off due to artillery fire. Suddenly, there was the sound of a twig cracking. The baby turned. A creature approached. It was a leopard. It had a shabby yellow fleece and irregular spots. It was old but a baby elephant was easy prey. It pounced but the baby moved slightly away. The baby bolted into a bush hoping the leopard would not find it.

BANG!!!

The leopard fell with a thud.

The baby peered over the bush and saw that two poachers had shot the leopard. Blood trickled into a puddle on the ground. The two humans skinned the beast, imitating what the coat would look like on them. When they left, the baby carried on ahead. It eventually came to an area called Elephants' Pass. As it wandered down the tarmac road there was an earth-shaking rumbling sound.

A tank was heading straight for the baby. The baby could not go round it and there was only sea on either side of the road. It could not swim but it jumped.

***

A few years later the conflict in the country ended. The baby was safe although it had seen the gore and traumatic deaths of humans and animals. The humans do not understand. Wars don't only affect them but also the wildlife. They also do not understand that the wars they wage cause more damage than they do good.

About the author

Lakshman Samarakoon was born in Middlesex and lives with his family in Pinner (London). His desire to increase awareness about the terrible impact of poaching and highlight the effects of war on not just humans but animals as well, inspired him to write the short story, *An Elephant's Journey*.

Lakshman attended St Martin's School, Northwood up until summer 2014 where he gained a scholarship to Merchant Taylor's School, Northwood. He enjoys reading books about World War I and II, for example, *The Book Thief* and *Eleven Eleven*.

Being an avid follower of Formula 1 motorsport, he would like to become a design engineer for a Formula 1 team. He also enjoys debating and was a member of the debating team at his former school. If design engineering does not work out he may well consider a career in politics!

Orcas *by Mairi Clayton*

About the artist

Mairi Clayton loves to draw, paint, read, and bake. She quite enjoys writing as well. She thinks Disney movies are tick

tick the bomb, and says that chocolate is always the answer. Mairi drew this picture of orcas in the wild after watching the documentary *Blackfish*, and reading a story her sister Darragh wrote about a young, captive killer whale. Mairi would encourage people not to visit animals like whales and dolphins in captivity, but donate to charities like Born Free which can help keep these creatures in their own habitats.

🐾 Paws for Thought Discussion Point

Mairi makes a very important point. The message from the Born Free Foundation is very clear: **whales and dolphins do not belong in tanks.** It makes grim reading what happens to these graceful, intelligent marine mammals when they're captured from the wild – for our 'entertainment'. They are forced to live in really nothing more than swimming pools when in the wild they would swim for hundreds, sometimes thousands of miles and live in large family groups. Many are starved so they'll 'perform well' in shows, doing anything for a piece of fish, and it's supposed to be fun! But is it fun for the dolphins and whales? Of course not.

In captivity, an artificial, unnatural and enclosed environment, life for a wild animal is extremely stressful and thus detrimental to their wellbeing. The stimulations of the wild: the interactions with the natural environment and other animal species do not exist, and this can have severe affects on the behaviour and wellbeing of a wild animal.

In captivity, dolphins and whales suffer from high mortality rates, low breeding success and often endure physical and psychological disorders, not documented in the wild. It is therefore not a surprise that there have been incidents at places like SeaWorld Orlando where people have died or been injured when interacting with the animals. In fact, it is surprising that more 'accidents' have not occurred."

Despite the obvious risks of injury or worse, the captive dolphin industry is encouraging members of the public to swim with and interact with dolphins and other marine mammals. Swimming with dolphins in a captive environment has become a global business for tour operators that sell "once in a lifetime opportunities". The physical risks involved are frequently ignored and what precautions are taken often focus on reducing the transmission of disease between the animals and the public.

The Born Free Foundation strongly urges that people do not swim with marine mammals. We need to be more aware of the suffering endured by captive dolphins and the risks to public health and safety.

Unfortunately, due to the demand by holidaymakers to swim with dolphins, in addition to the travel industry to supply the demand, the numbers of captive dolphin facilities are on the increase. Captive dolphin attractions have become 'must-haves' for tourist resorts, zoos and even hotels, and with captive dolphin populations in decline, wild dolphins are being captured from the wild to supply this demand. So it's up to you to make sure there is no demand for these places by boycotting them and making sure you get your friends to all do the same. It's time to put an end to this suffering once and for all. Look at the Born Free website to see how you can help.

The Leopard

Wynn Thomas

There is nothing more beautiful than an African sunrise, when a great ball of fire slowly makes its way through the horizon. The golden glow is awesome. The stillness and peace at dawn is magical, with the occasional trumpet of an elephant and the sound of birds drifting in and out on the gentle breeze. I laze in the low lying branches of an Acacia tree gazing over the Serengeti Plain, my tail twitching from side to side. I feel a burning as the rays of the sun start to warm my body. Soon it will be time to lick my spots, clean my paws and sharpen my claws ready for a day of hunting. I haven't eaten in six days.

There has been rainfall, so the game has not gathered by the waterhole, as it usually does. Normally I have lots of choice – warthog, impala, springbok, kudu. Normally I stalk my prey while they are drinking and unprepared for an attack. Normally I creep stealthily through the dry grass on my haunches, then explode into an attack and pin my prey to the ground. With a single bite, I crush the windpipe of the animal and wait for its final breath and for its body to go limp. It is then that I must work the hardest. I have to drag and lift a dead weight into the safety of my tree, away from the lions and hyenas that lurk in my territory, waiting to steal my catch.

I have spent thirteen years on the plain. When I was a young leopard, my strength was supreme. I could drag the heaviest impala into a tree, muscles bulging in my back legs. My jaw could tear apart the toughest of skins. In those days I needed a big catch to survive. Now I am weaker. I do not have that same strength. My prey is smaller and lighter, which means I need to hunt more often to survive.

Yesterday, I was on the scent of a warthog. As I crept nearer, the warthog, with its bad eyesight but keen sense of smell, realised I was closing in. The warthog was downwind – I am getting careless in my old age. With that it started to squeal and run. I wasn't going to give up the chase. I was starving. I carried on, twisting and turning my streamlined body, to keep up with its attempts to escape me. Closer and closer I came and, just when I thought it was safe to pounce, the warthog backed into a hole. I didn't see this coming and leapt past it, my hind leg catching the sharp end of the tusk. I could feel my skin tearing and the pain running through my body. I limped to the shade of a tree and nursed my wound, licking furiously at it, trying to stop the flow of blood. The scent of fresh blood in the Serengeti is not good when it is coming from you. With hungry animals close by, needing to feed their young, you can easily become prey. I had to get to a tree and quick. I limped to the nearest one by the river and heaved my body inch by inch up the trunk to safety, where I could slump and regain my strength. There I fell asleep, weakened by the loss of blood and lack of food.

Wakened by the sunrise, yesterday's events seem so long ago. I was dreaming that I was young and strong again, but now I realise I am in serious trouble. I need food and water. My energy has drained from my body and I am in no condition to hunt. If I descend the tree, I probably will not be able to get back up again. I try to clean myself. My rosettes, normally so bright, seem dull. I am listless and slump back down again. I have to gather all my strength just to move my body, but the pain is too much. I wince as I shift position. I see red blood trickling down the trunk of the tree. My vision is blurred. I lie and wait. It is not easy being a lone animal, as there is no one to offer help if you are in trouble. It is a lonely life on the plains.

Then I hear a light, laughing sound in the distance. It sounds happy and I start to feel my pain lifting. Help is on its way. As the laughing approaches, the familiar sounds of my enemy become clear – that rasping, hacking laughter. I open my one eye to gaze into the bush below, now white hot in the heat of the African sun. There, gathered below, is a group of hyenas, snouts raised to my limp body above, sniffing the scent of my blood. Next a vulture lands near the hyenas and a fight breaks out. There is a racket of sound as more vultures fly in and the hyenas defend their territory. I feel so weak. I place my paw over my face.

About the author

Wynn Thomas is British born of South African parents. His love of the bush has developed over thirteen years of visiting South Africa and the wonderful game farms there. He loves to play rugby, cricket, golf and tennis. His hobby is playing and collecting ukuleles.

He is heading to Sherborne in Dorset to start senior school and has dedicated this story to Boppie and Ma, his grandparents, who continue to inspire in him a love of nature and freedom of thought.

Years 9 – 11

A note from our judge, Michaela Strachan

Michaela Strachan is one of TV's best loved wildlife presenters. She has a huge amount of enthusiasm and compassion for animals. Michaela is probably best known for presenting wildlife programmes like: *The Really Wild Show*, *Michaela's Wild Challenge*, *Orangutan Diaries*, *Elephant Diaries*, *Animal Rescue Squad*, *Countryfile*, *Springwatch*, *Autumnwatch* and *Winterwatch*. Fans from the 80s will also remember *The Wide Awake Club*, and the cult late night show *The Hitman And Her*.

Michaela Strachan's *Really Wild Adventures* is a book of fun and factual animal rhymes about adventures she's had while filming wildlife.

This is what she said about the stories:

"I was absolutely bowled over by the standard of writing in this category. All five finalists wrote compelling, original and quite brilliant short stories. I was hugely impressed with the standard which made my job of choosing a winner pretty tricky! It was a really close call between first and second place but I went for Wriggling away from Wombattiness by Marisa Orton, because it was so quirky and original. It's a great animal to choose, one that most people have never heard of, and I loved it immediately from its wacky title

96

to its poignant end. The writer shows enormous promise of being quite a brilliant future novelist! Well done for coming up with something so original and unique.

The Tigress by Emily Wootton was an incredible and quite beautiful but sad story of the last tigress left. A huntress, survivor, a fighter. The descriptions of her are stunning and beautifully written. I loved the occasional rhyme in the story and I love some of the phrases. This is an exquisitely written tragic tale. An incredibly moving, poetic and mature short story. I loved it."

Winning Story: Years 9 – 11

Wriggling away from Wombattiness
Marisa Orton

The lusciously sweet scents of dewdrops, untouched undergrowth and fresh grass oscillated into one another, as the wind carried their gorgeous essence upon its breeze, the way a royal carriage would transport a princess to her castle. Only to be detected by one with a sharp enough sense of smell, the balm that came from a nearby freshwater stream felt so close that I could feel it gently tickling the tip of my tongue. I breathed in the melody of scents, as I charged through grass of a myriad different shades of emerald. Wading into the cool water and losing myself in the freshness that made all my worries sweep away into its unfathomable depths, I forgot everything except the freedom I suddenly felt. A sensation, like the rippling waves surrounding me, swept through my body, warming my heart and cleansing my fur. Sometimes I miss those days.

Those times before the world of Two-legs, as well as my own dear Animal Kingdom, knew about the Northern Hairy-Nosed Wombat. There was something to be said for a life of utter privacy; it's as if you're merely a passing cloud, watching the world from an omniscient view, but not actually being a part of it. My memory of such a state of mind had become blurred since my new life started, but I often wonder which path I would have chosen if I'd had the choice. I hardly knew what had happened when I was suddenly hauled, one bright morning, out of a peacefully cosy tree-trunk-cave by a pointy-nosed scientist. He had funny hair that stuck up in tufts around his head and transparent circles over his eyes. His nose, which indiscreetly poked itself into my shelter, put my elephant acquaintances to shame. He held me high above his head, prodded my stumpy legs, ruffled my fur and cried out an exclamation of undeniable joy. He flashed an unlikeable contraptional device in front of my nose and I squirmed desperately when it lit up abruptly, because I didn't like bright lights. Still, he didn't set me down until he'd cut a few hairs from my flank and seven more flashes had startled me. The next time I strayed into the forest after my recovery hibernation, I realised everything had changed after that large-nosed scientist discovered me.

Not only had he introduced the whole Two-leg world to my kind, but even within the Animal Kingdom, my status had changed. Suddenly a known species, the Northern Hairy-Nosed Wombat was a respected and dominant part of the world we inhabited. In a matter of moons, I was part of Congress (which was originally controlled solely by the purebred wolves) and was soon elected to be one of the king lion's first-hand officials. The lion, known by most as Mortimer, had been the leader of our kingdom for many long years. His great achievements had been magnificent, from his victory against a band of hunting Two-legs, to his unwavering success in raising every animal of the forest to be strong and fearless, just as he was. Mortimer was huge, even for a lion, and when he shook his great head from high up on the leader's stone ledge, it was as if he had us all hypnotised. There wasn't a creature in our jungle who didn't obey his every command. His pelt, well-kept and permanently glossy, was a sharp, honey-like colour, very much camouflaged against the harsh sands of distant deserts. Then, before I knew it, I was the one standing on that ledge.

Below me, every jungle animal was gathered, waiting expectantly for my instructions. The giraffes bowed their long necks, the tigers sat respectfully on their wide haunches, the ant-eaters ceased their endless search for insects, the birds listened from their precarious tree-top positions, the wolves of Congress who sat on lower stone ledges behowled the moon, to make sure every creature knew their leader was going to speak. Mortimer disappeared into the crowd obediently, his eyes dark as he curled his tail gently by his side. He was watching me carefully. And they were all waiting – waiting for this Northern Hairy-Nosed Wombat to take charge as he had been appointed to do. I scanned the scene around me. This was wrong – everything was out of place – and it was all because of me. Before that scientist had discovered me, no one, Two-leg or animal, had so much as heard of a creature like me, so what was I doing on the king's ledge? Why were all these animals gathered before me? The Way of the Wild hadn't planned for this to happen!

Mortimer should have been up there, roaring in a growl that soared high above the sounds of all the other jungle animals. The carnivores should have been chasing down their dinner; the unfortunate herbivores should have been avoiding their bared fangs. The birds should have been singing, high up above the treetops, in a world no one else would ever know. And I, the Northern Hairy-Nosed Wombat, should have been snoring lazily in my habitual tree-trunk, wading into the secret stream to bathe and sniffing out small insects in the undergrowth. I couldn't remember the last time I'd let my hairy nose bask in all the fresh scents of the jungle around me. Oh, how I missed tasting all those smells on my tongue! My stumpy legs making it hard for me to jump down from the ledge, I lowered my head and ignored the wolves' protests about my departure. I took one last look at the surrounding crowd of animals and then vanished into the olive-green bushes.

In the distance, I heard a ferocious roar and the sound of desperately pounding pawsteps fleeing from their oppressors. The Way of the Wild. I grunted in approval, because while it may have been cruel, that was the way things were supposed to be. I, however, slowly ambled down the never-trodden-before secret paths to the stream, unnoticed and never to be seen again. Just the way I liked it. I touched a paw to the water and felt its coolness.

About the author

Marisa Orton's favourite hobby, without a doubt, is writing. She won her first writing competition at the age of seven, with a theatre review of *The Snow Queen*. From short stories and novels to articles and book reviews, she loves writing in all forms and styles. She was born in England and has been living in France for five years now, an incredible experience, which is the reason she can now fluently speak French and English. She studies at an entirely French collège, living with her mum and playful cat, Emily, in a spectacular, mountain village in the south of France. Consequently, learning languages, tennis, splashing people at the pool and enjoying the great weather are favourite activities of hers.

🐾 Paws for Thought Discussion Point

So how much do you know about wombats? Can you draw one? The species in Marisa's story, the Northern Hairy-Nosed Wombat is one of the world's rarest large mammals and sadly, like so many animals you have read about here, is critically endangered. Threats to the Northern Hairy-Nosed Wombat include small population size, predation, competition for food, disease, floods, droughts, wildfires, and habitat loss. Having such small population sizes makes the species especially vulnerable to natural disasters. Wild dogs are probably the wombat's number one predator. The habitat at Epping Forest National Park in Australia is now well-protected to ensure better chances of survival. See what you can find out about wombats. How many species of wombat are there?

Runner-up

The Tigress
Emily Wootton

She is a tiger. Her fur is spectacular: an orange sunset
dappled with stripes black as the night sky. With the
moonlight streaming down – flooding the forest – her
pelt adopts an ethereal glow. Underneath the mass of fur,
muscles ripple in time with her movements. They carry the
fatigue of her journey. Gouging grooves into the ground,
ebony paws and ivory claws create a striking contrast.
Eyes of burnished gold stare worriedly, warily, wearily at
the path ahead; who knows what danger could be cloaked
in a veil of darkness? She is a huntress. Padding through
the forest she should be the epitome of magnificence. But
scars criss-cross her flank – reminders of past struggles.
Yet she has caused the demise of many others: be it by the
slash of claw or the clamp of jaw.

The instinct to hunt is deeply rooted within her. Prey
means food, and food means survival – and survival is
mandatory. She is a mother. Prey is even more necessary
with two extra mouths to feed. Memories flood the tigress'
mind: of still days and harsh nights; of tiny cubs and large
appetites; of cold bodies and warm milk. She had reared
her babies from birth, from minute bundles of fur.

The love and pride would never easily be forgotten.
That fusion of emotions still runs through her now, as

raw as the wounds on her shoulder. She is a mourner. A harsh winter coupled with human activity meant a severe prey shortage. News of 'retaliation killings' had long been sweeping through the forest, carried by the bleak winds. Although the risks were great, the desperation was greater. No mother could watch her babies starve to death. Little did she know the tales of retaliation killings were very much real. In mere seconds her cubs were shot dead, their blood streaking the ground, creating the illusion that their fur was melting before her very eyes. She is a fighter. Dried blood cakes her fur – like fresh paint on a canvas – bearing the pain of a thousand battles. She wears her scars like war paint; they are her personal trophies showing that she is an able warrior. But each freshly-inflicted wound delves deeper than the flesh and scourges her very soul. The tigress is damaged. She is a survivor. Though she leaves a trail of devastation behind her, against all odds, the tiger has survived. And she must. Weaving a path through the underbrush to find a safe haven. Away from the dank and the dark and the danger: survival is the only option. Anything else is superfluous. Bang! She is in danger. She hurtles through the trees like her life depends on it. (And it very much does.)

Adrenaline courses through her veins like liquid fire. The undergrowth flashes past, the colours merging, blurring into one. Bullets fly past her, the shots reverberating in her ears so the ominous thunder of bullets is all she hears. They ricochet off the trees, impaling branches and sending them to the floor. The tiger knows that if she does not run, she will be those branches. She is safe. After a lifetime of running, the tigress has outdistanced the danger. The silence that engulfs the clearing is strangely eerie now she is away from the threat of the guns. But they are gone. Bathing in the sunrise that heralds the birth of a new day, the tiger savours the tranquillity. The morning carries a newfound innocence which seemingly calms the whole forest. But she knows that sometime, sooner or later, she will be on the run again. Her life is an endless cycle of descent. However the tiger grants herself some rest – it is a rarity, and she has had little of it. She places her head on her paws, instantly falling to the mercy of another entity: sleep. She is a tiger. And she is the last one left...

Tiger *by Liah Clayton*

About the author

Emily Wootton is fifteen and lives on the south coast of England with her parents and, as an animal lover, three cats: Disney, Misty and Molly. She wanted to write the story to raise awareness of how human activity is affecting not just the tiger population, but many animal species across the world. She hopes that, one day, there will be no species of animal classed as endangered!

About the artist

Liah Clayton is ten years old and lives in PEI, Canada. This winter, she went to an art class and was inspired to start drawing and painting at home. Liah loves the numbers 5 and 3, but is not a fan of 6 or 7! She also loves candy and ballet, as well as animals, of course. She thinks people should stop hunting animals like white tigers and snow leopards, and other endangered species. In her opinion, animals should live their own life, and be Wild n Free!

Snow Baby
Bethany Dale

The sun remained low in the sky as snow fell down quickly, swirling down in great flurries. The harsh wind whipped across the land while the Arctic Ocean crashed against the shore. A young seal jumped from an iceberg and landed in the sea, using its tail as a rudder to dive down deeper where it would be warmer than on land. Penguins also waddled by with their flippers over their head to keep the snow away from their eyes. However, the harsh weather did not bother all the animals... deep inside a perfectly dug snow den sat the world's largest land carnivore. A polar bear.

Her fur was thick and hung over her body like a coat. She was completely white apart from her soft brown eyes and black button nose. The bear's body was so large that she took up most of the room inside the den but there was just enough space for her cub to squeeze in beside her. It was more than half the size of its mother and was snuggled into the warmth of her fur.

"What are we doing today, Mother?" the cub asked, "Can we go outside and play?"

"It's February still! The weather is too cold for a little thing like you."

"I'm not little! I've grown lots over the winter," the

little polar bear said, pointing at the height chart scrawled on the den wall. There were little marks that showed the cub's height at different ages.

The mother polar bear looked down at the first mark showing the cub's height at birth to be 30cm, no bigger than a human foot. She remembered the tiny ball of helpless fluff with fur so fine that it appeared bald. She had never felt that kind of love for anything before and now it was just the two of them together, safe from the world in their den. However, not all of her kind was so safe. Mother polar bear had heard the stories of the ice melting too early in the summer so the pregnant bears didn't have enough time to hunt for food before giving birth. She had been lucky to find lots of seals to eat and put on weight so she wouldn't have to hunt when she was nursing her baby. She was scared about the future of the Arctic and what it held for her little cub when it grew older. However hard it was to be a wild animal she knew that she was better off than those who were held captive at zoos. Beaten, abused, and starved, were just the start of the stories she had heard. Now every time she saw a falling star she would wish that they could be let back into the wild so that they could be free like her. No animal should have to live in a cage; wild animals are born free after all.

***

It was April. The days had lengthened rapidly with the sun rising high in the sky on most days. The little cub had grown quickly too and was now ready to make an appearance. His mother crawled to the entrance of their den and pushed the snow covering it aside. A bright jet of light seeped down into the hole, almost blinding the polar bear cub. His first glimpse of daylight! The female stuck her nose out of the hole and sniffed the air. When she thought it was safe she edged out of the den and looked at the deserted ice land around her. Everything was covered in a thin layer of snow and although the sun was out there was still a frosty chill that buried itself deep into her coat. "Don't be afraid," she whispered to her cub who was still sitting inside the den. He took a few cautious steps forwards before scrambling up beside his mother. The snow crunched underneath his padded feet and left little paws prints.

"Go on!" Mother polar bear encouraged the cub, pushing him forward with her nose. The baby polar bear suddenly lost his balance and landed face down in the snow. He got up quickly, shaking the snow off himself. Wait... this is actually quite fun, he thought to himself, and began to roll around in the soft snow, occasionally sneezing as it went up his nose. "I'm free!" the cub shouted over and over again as he got up and started to run around, kicking snow up with his feet.

His mother watched from a distance. Her stomach rumbled and she remembered that she had not eaten for many months. It was time to go hunting. She took one more look at the den where she and her baby had spent many days and nights together. It was now time to move on. She looked away and back at her cub. He was still playing happily in the snow ahead of her and she smiled. "My little snow baby," she whispered into the Arctic air. The two bears' coats acted as camouflage against the snow as they walked into the distance, side by side, to face the world together.

About the author

Bethany Dale has lived in Essex all her life. She is a passionate writer, bookworm and animal enthusiast. Bethany has also been a dedicated supporter of the Born Free Foundation for many years. She lives with her tabby cat called Toby, who constantly reminds her how much he loves her by catching the odd mouse or two.

One day she would love to travel to Africa to see the big cats and other wild animals in their natural habitat, where they belong.

The Hunt
Keira Layton

"Mama," whined the Tiger cub, "when will Jay and Father be back?"

Luna was crouched low, her belly fur brushing the dry bracken on the floor. Her wide green eyes scanned the clearing, until they rested on a dead leaf, fluttering around in the wind, like a confused moth. She tensed her hind legs, and pouncing, landed just short of it, a gust of wind snatching it away; tossing it just out of her reach, as if taunting her. Her mother glanced up from the flat rock she was sunning herself on.

"They'll be back once they have caught dinner," her mother mumbled, her orange and black tail swishing gently, sweeping up a cloud of dust. Luna shivered. The clearing felt cold and empty without her brother and father. She missed all the luscious green leaves that normally fringed it, and the bright berries that brought down the birds for her to catch. She never did, but was certain she would one day. She would have to, if spring took much longer to come. All the larger prey was scarce anyway, because the humans kept taking it. Suddenly, a figure threw itself into the clearing, and collapsed heavily on the floor.

"Jay!" shouted Luna, as she rushed towards her trembling brother. "What happened?" Her mother crouched beside him, licking his fluffy ears furiously. Blood flowed from a deep gash in his paw, creating a sticky red puddle. He could remember only too well what had happened... Hissssssss. Jay heard his father in the bush next to him. He had seen something! He opened his mouth, and let the musty forest scents overwhelm him. There it was – the scent of rabbit. Some dry leaves rustled, and a furry brown head poked out of a hole in the ground. That must be its burrow, Jay thought. A rabbit would be barely enough to feed tiny Luna, but they had been hunting for hours and found nothing. It would have to do. A few leaves shifted in the canopy, catching Jay's eye. It's probably just a bird he thought, focusing his attention back on his prey. The rabbit bounded forwards to nibble on a seed. Jay's paws itched to leap, but he knew that if he attacked too soon, the rabbit would dash out of his grasp and into cover before he could say 'prey'.

Suddenly, a stone fell from the branches of the tree above it, killing it instantly. Two figures leapt from the tree. "Humans!" spat Jay angrily. Humans were always stealing their prey. A low growl from his father warned him to stay hidden. One of the humans was tall, and Jay guessed he was an adult, but the other was smaller and thinner, he must be a child. The child had dark matted hair which hung around his face like wet ivy. "Good kill, Luka," the adult praised the child, who had dragged the limp rabbit from under the stone, which was now spattered with blood. Jay hissed angrily. That was to be his catch, not theirs. All of a sudden, the humans stopped dead, and scanned the clearing. They'd heard him.

"Tiger! We could do with some extra money from their pelts!" He barked an order to the child who passed him a long, metal spear. He began stabbing into each bush with it, trying to drive them out. Jay caught his father's eye, who nodded, and they streaked out of the bush like lightning, pelts brushing. The humans shouted and gave chase, leaping over streams and rocks. Brambles tore at Jay's pelt, leaving clumps of ginger fur for the humans to follow. Jay ducked under a huge cobweb, strung between two trees. A perfectly placed trap. The humans ran straight into it, and silver strands enveloped their faces. They spluttered as cobweb floated into their mouths, sticking to their teeth. He wanted to turn, and watch the humans, usually superior, halted by a mere spider web, but there was no time. He had to keep running. Something caught his paw, it tore at the skin. Blood spattered the brown leaves. Pain jolted through his leg, but he kept on running. He had to keep on running. Movement in the sky caught his eye. Something arced gracefully above him like a bird, making a quiet, whistling sound. The humans' spear! It dived down, and he heard a thud, the kind of thud that was made by a spear stabbing flesh. His father! Jay dived into a bush and peered out cautiously.

He was hidden here, but he wouldn't be safe for long. He could see a body, with ginger fur and a tail lying on the floor like a dead snake. Scarlet blood had gushed from a huge puncture in its side, where the spear stuck. Jay froze in horror. His father had been killed. Pain and sadness tore at his heart. The humans ran up to the body and cheered. They kicked and prodded the lifeless mound of fur, taunting it cruelly. Eventually, they grabbed its legs, and heaved it out of the forest, its tail scoring a thin line in the dusty mud on the floor. His father was dead. He couldn't feel the pain in his paw, the ache of his lungs.

He couldn't feel anything anymore. Jay bolted home, his heart heavy with grief. Now he lay with his sister, his mother licking him rapidly. Glancing up at them, he saw tears glistening in their eyes.

"He's gone," Jay murmured solemnly, barely loud enough for the others to hear. "I can't believe he's really gone."

"Who's gone?" asked a voice, and his father's head poked round a bush. Jay stared in disbelief. He had seen him lying there, covered in blood, limp and lifeless. This couldn't be possible. "The foolish humans didn't kill me," his father commented, after taking a moment to get his breath back. "No, they didn't get me this time. You know when your grandpa died last week in the forest, and we left him to rest in a clearing?"

Luna and Jay nodded, not knowing how this had any relevance with the current subject.

"Well, the spear hit his body, and those bird-brained humans thought it was me!"

Jay smiled, his paw forgotten, the humans would never learn. Humans and Tigers would never live together in peace.

About the author

Keira Layton lives in Heckmondwike, West Yorkshire, and attends Heckmondwike Grammar School. She loves to write both poetry and prose, and has been published as a result of several previous competitions. She loves to play with her two cats: Bugsy and Lilly, and also enjoys drama, procrastinating on the internet and gaming with friends.

A self-proclaimed Goth, she chooses to wear all black

and listen to rock music. Refusing to be conventional, she interjects the word 'cheese' into conversations at any given moment, always injures herself in the most bizarre and obscure ways, and has a fear of stickers.

Tiger *by Morgan Joy Ashby (cover artist)*

Goshawk – Life in the Trees

Dominik Reynolds

As I sat on the edge of my nest, the wind rustling my feathers, the soft mossy bark under my talons, I wondered how many times over the years I had swooped among the branches of these towering trees, whilst picking off a lone pigeon or squirrel, and how many times I would do so in years to come. The nest, the colossal nest, had its disadvantages. Roughly thirty-five feet above the ground, a fall would surely kill any small chick. But no matter what the weather, whatever time of year, food was nearly always in good supply in these parts of the woods. Many times I had fought off rivals, all fighting for this prime spot. But this nest was my creation, and for three years mine it had remained.

I looked back into the nest, my eyes resting on my precious three eggs. As long as they were there, nothing else mattered. Not even my partner could get in the way of my maternal bond to the eggs. I seemed to gaze around my nest, at my brood, for an eternity, listening to the many sounds of the forest above and below, when suddenly a piercing shriek echoed through the canopy. My head snapped round, and following another cry, I saw the silhouette of a Goshawk arc around and swoop down towards the nest. My partner had returned. As he landed, I saw the blood on his beak and knew his hunt had been successful. I hoped mine would be too. We looked each other up and down in greeting and he carefully nestled down covering the eggs. With a quick screech, I launched myself over the side and soared off into the woods in search of prey.

***

Two weeks later, a storm was raging over the forest. The wind buffeted my sides, threatening to throw me out of the nest. Gales blustered throughout the woods, making even the tallest and strongest of trees sway. The rain came down in heavy sheets, and I was soaked through to my skin. As the wind continuously picked up and then dropped again, the deafening roars and terrible cracking of the trees terrified me. Even though my nest was in a strong larch tree, I could feel the branch lurching back and forth.

I huddled lower, trying to shelter my chicks. They were growing at a fair rate, and now they were starting to lose their fluffy downy feathers. But still, even though I knew I had to focus on my two chicks, I couldn't help feeling some sorrow towards the third egg that hadn't hatched. It had been torture to tip it over the side of the nest and watch it fall to the ground. I didn't know its fate, because the next day it had gone. But I still had two healthy chicks, and I had to focus on their future.

Suddenly I was distracted from my thoughts when a particularly strong gust blew me head on. I shifted off one of the chicks, and it cried out. I carefully got up to try and rearrange myself when a gale struck my chest, and I keeled backwards. I looked up and saw the chicks trying to hunker down. I screeched in horror, and then the nest left my feet and I was falling. I stuck out my wings, and luckily the wind lifted me. I regained control and struggling against the wind, I swooped back to the nest. I landed and to my relief I found they were both OK, both still in the centre of the nest, bedraggled but unharmed. In a break in the wind, I hastily covered the chicks, then put my head under my wing and tried to sleep against the howling storm.

The forest floor was crawling with all kinds of life, scavenging food from collapsed trees and the leaf-ridden earth. It had been two days since the storm had torn through my home, but still there were mice, squirrels, rats and many birds all feeding from the remnants of the destruction. My keen eyes were scanning for a suitable meal for my chicks, as they were always the priority. I would eat part of whatever I caught, but the chicks would need the majority of the meat. I was looking around the canopy when my eyes locked onto a group of pigeons that were sat in the lower branches of a pine tree not far from the nest. I crouched down and got ready to go.

One of the chicks wailed and hobbled over, but I pushed it back and gave it a return screech of my own. Then, after one last look at my chicks, I launched over the edge.

The forest floor came rushing at me, and I felt the wind ruffling my feathers. I never felt better than whenever I went hunting. At the last second I pulled up sharply, and then I was flying along above the floor. With a few beats of my great wings, I was up in the canopy, swooping through the branches. I made a few passes before I found the pigeons again, cooing amongst each other. I circled their location in silence, finding an easy route through the leaves and branches. When I thought I had found one, I circled round once more just to make sure, then I folded back my wings and dived towards my prey.

I was going straight for them. They had no idea that I, the deadliest air predator in the forest, was heading straight for them. I stretched my legs forward and readied my talons, but then one turned around and saw me. Its eyes widened in terror and it let out a horrible squawk. As soon as it flew off, the others followed immediately. They scattered in all directions and I barrelled through them. I had to swerve to avoid a tree, and I circled round to see where they were going. Most of them were in a group, but one was on its own. It was far away, but I wasn't giving up, I could not give up. I swooped round and went after it. It must have heard me coming, because it started darting left and right. I followed after it, but the branches became thinner. The pigeon flew through a fork in a tree, thinking it would lose me, but I knew I would fit, and my chicks needed feeding. So I folded my wings and stretched my legs forward. I felt the bark pass beside me as I went through at top speed. I soared up above the trees, waiting for a chance to strike from above. When I saw the pigeon beneath the branches, I waited for a gap in the canopy, then I went for it, talons outstretched. I narrowed my eyes against the stinging wind. It tried to swerve away, but my talons dug in, and it was snatched out of the air. Triumphantly, I turned to fly back to my nest, my head raised high, my prize in my grasp.

***

The chicks were becoming more and more restless as the days went on. They were not the small, white, fluffy chicks they once were. They were almost fully grown now, displaying rich brown feathers and they were starting to grow bold, hopping closer to the nest edge, even onto the adjacent branches. I had known that fledging day had been coming, as the chicks had been stretching and flapping, strengthening their wings for a few days.

Even though I knew that it had to happen, I was still very nervous for the chicks. However, they seemed to be very confident, and they were screeching and squawking as they ventured ever further out from the nest. Suddenly one of the chicks bounced up to the edge of a thick branch and stood there, looking uneasy. I could tell it was unsure. It looked back at me and cried out, shuffling its feet. I returned the cry, and it turned back and looked out into the forest. After what seemed like forever, it stretched out its wings and dropped out of view. I hurried over to the side of the nest and peered over, and then I saw the chick soaring off into the forest. As I felt my other chick dive off into the forest beside me I felt a little sad, but also overjoyed that, after all my hard work, both of the chicks had survived and had successfully left the nest. I watched their silhouettes merge into the forest. However, it wasn't the last time I saw them. For a while after their fledging, they returned for food at various times. Sometimes they even spent the night in the nest before departing again. Then they were gone.

My life was my own again. Free to enjoy the wild forest, until next year.

About the author

Dominik Reynolds, fourteen, lives in Totton on the edge of the beautiful New Forest. Dominik loves all wildlife and since the age of nine he has worked as a volunteer, on weekend and holidays, for the RSPB on their Date with

Nature Project in the forest and his passion for goshawks came through his volunteering, making this stunning bird an easy choice for his story. He plans to study Zoology in the future and wants to work in conservation. At home he has a cat, Zizi, and two Giant African Land Snails. He enjoys writing, reading, karate and acting but is at his happiest in the Great Outdoors.

🐾 Paws for Thought Discussion Point

Do you know anything about goshawks? What wonderful birds of prey they are. See if you can find out more about them.

The Paws Writing Competition
Your chance to be published

Thank you for reading this very special book and we hope you enjoyed it and that it brings you a little closer to understanding the emotions of wild animals. All the children I think have really captured this. It is amazing how varied the stories are.

If, like the children who entered the Paws Competition, you are also a child that loves to write or you're the parent or teacher of a child that does, then why not enter the competition yourself or encourage your child to.

We plan to run the Paws Writing Competition again although it might now be every two or three years so sign up for the newsletter on the website below to keep informed!

www.pawsnclawspublishing.co.uk

Paws for Thought
Discussion Points
– a note for teachers and parents

The questions in this book – further discussion

Throughout the book, I have included questions and suggested that children might like to find out more about some of the animals they have read about. We hope some of the questions, and other questions that arise while reading this book, will lead to further discussion. And we really hope children will want to know more about the animals they've read about and do some of their own research, maybe even write their own story. We would love for schools/groups to really embrace some of the questions raised in this book.

If you would like to take that a step further and take part in a PAWS workshop then do check out our website and talk to your schools. Does your school have trips to the zoo? Have you thought about the animals in zoos and wildlife parks? Are they really there to make money or do they really put a lot of money into conservation? With the majority of zoos it's so much smaller than you might think.

Do you think we should have zoos? Perhaps you might even encourage your school to have an alternative to the zoo trip? Perhaps you would like one of these workshops instead?

To find out more about PAWS visit the Paws n Claws website:

www.pawsnclawspublishing.co.uk/PAWSWorkshopScheme

Index

*(Page numbers in **bold type** refer to illustrations)*

Aldridge-Bate, Charlie, 14
Amrani, Adam, 17, **20**
Amrani, Sophien, 21, **24**
Ashby, Morgan Joy, xiii, **8, 65, 115**
Clayton, Liah, **105**
Clayton, Mairi, **90**
Cleak, Xander, 1
Cooper, Vienna, 51
Cumming, Alex, 57
Cumming, Thomas, 26, **28**
Cuthbert, Daisy, 9
Dale, Bethany, 107
Forshew, Jack, 29
Freeman, Maia, 47
Gadsdon, Henry, 60
Hartwell, Tristan, 32
Hilton, Honey, 63
Hobbs-Wyatt, Debz, ix, xi

Jenkins, Teddy, 35
Lakhani, Tayin, 66, **75**
Layton, Keira, 111
Madan, Manas, 69
McCarthy, Emma, 38
Nair, Vivek, 41, **43**
Orton, Marisa, 98
Radtke, Nicole, **50**
Ratnam, Ryan, 77
Reynolds, Dominik, 116
Rochussen, Thomas, 83
Samarakoon, Lakshman, 87
Spedding, Sally, 45
Strachan, Michaela, 96
Tenbeth, Kate, xv
Thomas, Wynn, 93
Warnock, Tristan, 4
Wootton, Emily, 103

Other Books by Paws n Claws that help wild animals

Jet-Set

Paws n Claws Publishing specialise in fictional books about animals and every book makes a donation to the Born Free Foundation.

To find out more about us visit our website:
www.pawsnclawspublishing.co.uk

To find out more about The Jet-Set and to sign up for our fun animal newsletter visit: *www.thejet-set.com*

If you want to learn about the Born Free Foundation and their children's Wild Crew Club visit:
http://www.bornfree.org.uk/kids-go-wild/wildcrew/

Born Free Foundation's
Wild About Animals

ISBN: 978-0-9568939-8-7

Featuring Winning Poems from
Born Free Foundation's 30th Anniversary Children's Poetry
Competition judged by Pam Ayres, Brian Patten, Lauren St John,
Richard Bonfield, Virginia McKenna and Debz Hobbs-Wyatt

Poems by children from around the world, a wonderful
companion to *Wild n Free Forever*

Copies of the book can be purchased from the
Born Free Foundation's online shop – give.bornfree.org.uk
and usual online retailers

Wild n Free

Winner and Runners-up from the first Paws Animal Writing
Competition for Children with judges Virginia McKenna OBE,
Lauren St John and Alan Gibbons.
Written and illustrated by children aged 9 – 16.

All royalties to the Born Free Foundation

ISBN: 978-0-9568939-4-9

Order from Amazon, other online retailers
and from local bookshops

Wild n Free Too

Winner and Runners-up from the second Paws Animal
Writing Competition for Children with judges Daniel Blythe,
Kate Humble and Gill Lewis.
Written and illustrated by children aged 9 –16.

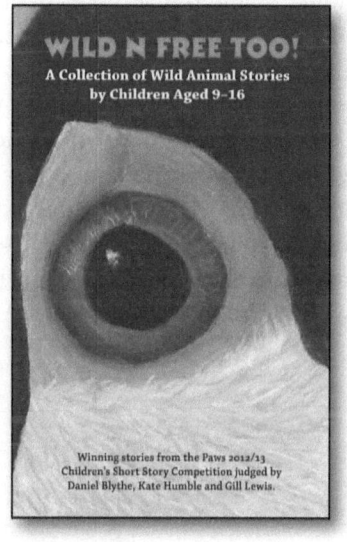

All royalties to the Born Free Foundation

ISBN: 978-0-9568939-6-3

Order from Amazon, other online retailers
and from local bookshops

Other books you might enjoy...

Hipp-O-Dee-Doo-Dah
For children

You'll find all sorts of animals in this collection of stories – a hippo
who longs for water, a chimp that proves to be tougher than a
gorilla, a horse only two people can see, a cat that cooks, a starfish
that falls from the sky and dogs that save lives.

There are some amazing people too – the young girl who
looks after her mum, some young people who have magical
powers they have to hide, a boy who finds a new way to remember
his grandfather, and a young man who has the universe at his
command but daren't let others see.

All of the stories are about how people are thoughtful with
each other or with the animals in their care. And they'll bring
sunshine to a grey day.

Hipp-O-Dee-Doo-Dah features stories by Blue Peter Award winners
Lauren St John and Alan Gibbons, and a foreword by Michael
Morpurgo OBE.

£1 from the sale of each copy, plus a percentage of the author
royalties, will be donated to Children's Hospices UK
(now Together for Short Lives)

ISBN 978-1-907335-11-2

Order from Amazon, bookshops or *www.bridgehousepublishing*.co.uk

Gentle Footprints
Edited by Debz Hobbs-Wyatt

Animal Short Stories (but written for adults so this book contains some adult language)

Gentle Footprints is a wonderful collection of short stories about wild animals. The stories are fictional but each story gives a real sense of the wildness of the animal, true to the Born Free edict that animals should be born free and should live free. The animals range from the octopus to the elephant, each story beautifully written. Gentle Footprints includes a new and highly original story by Richard Adams, author of Watership Down, and a foreword by the patron of Born Free, Virginia McKenna OBE.

£1 from the sale of each copy, plus a percentage of the author royalties, will be donated to the Born Free Foundation.

As featured on Mariella Frostrup's Book Show at Hay, 2010 and on ITV's *Loose Women*

ISBN 978-1-907335-04-4

Order from Amazon, bookshops or *www.bridgehousepublishing.co.uk*

www.ingramcontent.com/pod-product-compliance
Lightning Source LLC
Chambersburg PA
CBHW050822180626
46814CB00004B/1419